Letters
from
Hillside
Farm

Letters
from
Hillside Farm

Jerry Apps

FULCRUM
GOLDEN, COLORADO

Text © 2013 Jerry Apps

Library of Congress Cataloging-in-Publication Data on file

Printed in the United States of America
0 9 8 7 6 5 4 3 2 1

Design by Jack Lenzo

Fulcrum Publishing
4690 Table Mountain Dr., Ste. 100
Golden, CO 80403
800-992-2908 • 303-277-1623
www.fulcrumbooks.com

Introduction

The years 1929 to 1941 were known as the Great Depression in the United States. During that time millions of workers lost their jobs, and many families were uprooted as they moved from one part of the country to another. In the fictional Struckmeyer family, father Adolph Struckmeyer loses his factory job in Cleveland, Ohio, and moves with his wife and two children to a rundown rented farm in central Wisconsin. They borrow enough money from Grandma Struckmeyer to buy a few animals and necessary farm equipment. Adolph grew up on a farm, but his wife, Emily, twelve-year-old son George, and three-year-old daughter Annie know nothing about farm life until their move to Wisconsin.

When families moved, they often left behind grandparents and other relatives, as the Struckmeyer family does in this story. In the days before email and the Internet, letter-writing was the best way to keep in touch with family members left behind. This book is made up of the letters that young George Struckmeyer writes to his grandmother, whom he loves dearly and misses deeply, and the letters that Grandmother Struckmeyer writes back to George.

In his letters George describes life on the farm and at a one-room country school just as they were in the 1930s in many Midwestern farm communities. Few homes or schools had electricity or central

1

heating. Most farm work was done with horse and people power. People had little money, yet farms provided a ready source of food, and neighbors were always there to support one another.

March 15, 1938
Tuesday
Rural Route 1
Link Lake, Wisconsin

Dear Grandma,

We got here yesterday, and not an hour too soon. Since we were pulling the trailer behind our car, Pa couldn't drive very fast. As we crossed into Wisconsin and headed north, I saw snowflakes. I told Pa it's supposed to be spring, but he said that here in Wisconsin it can snow any month of the year. I think he was stretching the truth a little, but those surely were snowflakes that I saw. Little Annie said they were pretty, but she says that about everything.

Ma didn't say anything. I think she was tired. I know I was. It's a long drive from Cleveland, Ohio, to Link Lake, Wisconsin. By the time we pulled into the driveway at Hillside Farm—that's the name on the sign by the road—it had already snowed an inch or so and was coming down so hard Pa could scarcely see out the windshield of our old Plymouth. The windshield wipers made a kind of clunky sound as they pushed the snow aside. By the time we unloaded the car and the trailer, it was snowing so hard you couldn't see from one building to another.

While we were carrying things into the house, Pa told us that this is the beginning of a Great Adventure and that no matter what happens, we should always look at the sunny side of things.

I understand the adventure business. Pa has been talking about how this move to Wisconsin will be a Great Adventure ever since he and Ma started talking about leaving Ohio. But look on the sunny side, in the midst of a snowstorm?

So I thought about the puppy he promised to buy me, back when I raised a fuss about moving to a farm in faraway Wisconsin. But today when I asked him when I can get the puppy, he just laughed and said, "First things first."

The next thing I discovered about our Great Adventure is that it doesn't include indoor toilets! When I asked Pa where the bathroom is, he kind of smiled and said he saw it out back of the house when we first drove up. I asked him to show me where it is. So much snow was falling and the wind was blowing so hard that I could see just a few feet in front of my face. Pa walked with me to the outhouse, and even he had trouble finding the way. Can you imagine getting lost in a snowstorm trying to find your way to the bathroom?

Do you know what an outhouse is, Grandma? It's a little building with a door in the front and a kind of bench with holes in it where you can sit. When you drop your trousers and sit over one of the holes, you about freeze your backend. And there isn't even toilet paper. You use pages from an old Sears, Roebuck and Co. catalog! I tell you, you do what needs to be done and get out of there as fast as you can. It doesn't smell very nice, did I mention that? I was worried that I might fall through one of the holes. That would be just about the worst thing that could happen to anybody.

When I stepped into the kitchen of our new farmhouse, I saw Ma staring at the sink. There are no faucets! I asked Pa if we have running water. Do you know what he said? He said, "Sure we have running water—just go out to the pump house, pump a pail full, and run back to the house." Then he laughed. I didn't think it was funny, especially because Pa knows I can't run at all since I broke my leg last year. I think he must have forgotten about my limp. He never mentions it. Ma talks about it, though. She's always asking me if my leg hurts. It doesn't hurt much, only when I walk on it a lot. Ma is still upset with the doctor who tried to fix my leg. He didn't do a very good job of it. I guess the break was pretty bad. You wouldn't think you could break your leg falling out of a tree, but I sure did. The doctor said it will take a while for the leg to heal. How long is "a while?" It has already been three months.

One of the first things Pa did when we got inside was to start the fires in the kitchen and dining room stoves. That's how our house is heated, Grandma, with wood-burning stoves. There's a woodpile just a few steps from the west side of the house. Pa says one of my chores will be toting wood from the woodpile into the house, where I'm supposed to stack it in a wood box that stands beside each stove.

Ma has to do all the cooking on the wood-burning stove in the kitchen. She hasn't said so, but I'll bet she doesn't think much of that idea.

Tomorrow Pa's going to drive me to school and see about getting me enrolled. I have already missed a week since we left Ohio, and I am worried about falling behind. Seventh grade is not an easy year—at least, it wasn't in Ohio. I suspect it won't be easy here in Wisconsin, either. I am worried about going to a country school where all eight grades are in one room with one teacher. In the city the seventh and eighth grade students have their own room, with their own teacher. I'm also worried about my leg and whether I'll be able to walk to school. It's a mile from our farm.

This letter is my first chance to try out the writing paper and pencils you gave me. Ma says I must be sure to say thanks for such a fine present—so, thank you very much. I will try very hard to write to you as often as I can and let you know how I am doing in this new place.

I have also found a spot in my room for the leather tools you gave me. I hope I will have time to work on some new leather projects.

Ma is calling me to fetch some more water, so I must stop writing. I hope I can find my way to the pump house without getting lost in the snowstorm. We all miss you, Grandma. Little Annie keeps asking for you and wonders where you are. I guess she's too little to know that you are not just around the corner like you were in Ohio. I sure wish you were here. I wish we hadn't left Cleveland.

Love,
George

March 17, 1938
Thursday

Dear Grandma,

After the big snow I wrote to you about, we couldn't go anywhere until the snowplow struggled past our farm and plowed us out. That meant I didn't go to school until today. Our first day here we shoveled paths to the pump house, to the outhouse, to the woodshed, and from the car shed to the road. Pa said there'd be a lot more shoveling if we had cows and chickens and had to shovel our way to the barn and the chicken house.

Today Pa drove me to school and came and got me, too. The schoolhouse is a rickety, little, faded white building with no electricity, a woodstove, and outdoor toilets—one for the boys and one for the girls. There are only twenty students in the whole school. I am the only one in seventh grade. Miss Harvey, our teacher, is a tall, thin woman with black hair, long bony fingers, and eyes that stare right through you. She teaches all eight grades, besides making sure we do our duties. One of the duties Miss Harvey assigned to me is to carry in kindling wood from the woodshed each day. More wood carrying! The woodshed is a small red building not far from the schoolhouse. It is piled high with oak wood chunks and pine kindling for starting the fire in the schoolhouse stove.

Miss Harvey has everyone doing something. The first-graders pound the dust from the blackboard erasers. Older kids carry water from the pump house to fill the water cooler that stands at the back of the schoolroom. Kids that have been especially good at doing their duties over the years and stay out of trouble get to put up and take down the flag each morning and afternoon. The flag flies from a pole in the schoolyard near the front gate.

I don't know if I'll like this school or not. Pa keeps reminding me that school, too, is part of the Great Adventure.

Your grandson,
George

March 18, 1938
Friday

Dear Grandma,

Today I started walking to school on my own. It's only a mile, and the hills are not too steep. With all the fresh snow on the ground, I spotted some rabbit tracks. The snowstorm didn't seem to slow down the rabbits any.

Pa said it is an easy walk to the schoolhouse, but between my bad leg and stopping to inspect the rabbit tracks, I was a little late arriving at school. Well, you'd think I had committed a crime. When Miss Harvey saw me come in the door, she told me to hang up my coat and come up to her desk. She has a tone to her voice worse than Pa when he's mad. When I got up to her desk, she laid into me. In a voice loud enough that everybody in the school could hear, she said that nobody is ever late at Rose Hill School. She actually said it twice. While she was giving me a going-over, the rest of the kids were snickering and covering their mouths so Miss Harvey wouldn't see. I suspect if she had caught any of them laughing, she would have given them a talking-to as well.

I told Miss Harvey that I broke my leg last year—that it isn't right yet and keeps me from walking fast. She said that doesn't matter. She said if I can't walk fast I should leave home a little earlier. She doesn't seem to understand what it's like to have a gimpy leg.

Grandma, here it is, only my second day of classes, and I'm in trouble with the teacher. For punishment, she said I have to sweep out the boy's outhouse every morning and afternoon for two weeks!

Things got worse at recess. We were all outside in the schoolyard, getting ready to play a game Miss Harvey calls anti-I-over. Half the kids line up on one side of the little red woodshed, the other half on the other side. All that's needed to play the game is a rubber ball. A kid throws the ball over the woodshed while yelling "anti-I-over." The ball is supposed to bounce at least once on the opposite side of the building's roof. If someone on the other side of the building catches the ball, everyone on that side runs around to the other side. The kid who caught the ball tries to tag a kid on the other side, either by touching the kid or throwing the ball at him. If he succeeds, the kid who is touched by the ball joins the other team. The game goes on until one side captures all the players from the other side.

I had never heard of this game, but it sounded like it would be fun. I must have been standing there looking dumb, because just then Amos Woodward (he's an eighth-grader) stepped up to me and said that everyone should call me Limpy Late. Then he said, "We don't like city kids in our school, especially when they limp in after school starts." He was practically snarling, Grandma!

Amos Woodward is taller than I am, with arms that look like fence posts and a head that seems stuck straight to his shoulders, with no neck. His brown hair looks like it hasn't seen a comb for days, if ever.

I wanted to tell mister bigmouth Woodward to shut up, but I thought better of it. He'd probably pop me one in the choppers, and then I'd really be in trouble with Miss Harvey.

I noticed that Amos was staring at my leather belt—the one with all the designs on it that you showed me how to make. He asked me where I got it, and I told him that I made it. He said he didn't believe me. Before I had a chance to answer, Miss Harvey said there would be no bickering. So I kept my mouth shut.

This was not a good day. The only good part was learning a new game.

Love,
George

Cleveland, Ohio

Dear George,

Your letter of March 15 arrived today. I'm so happy to know that you all arrived in Wisconsin safe and sound. I know it must be disappointing to not have electricity, to have to go to the bathroom in an outhouse, and to warm your house with wood-burning stoves. But do you remember what I told you about what it was like when I was a little girl? In case you don't remember all the details, I'll share some of them again.

I grew up on a farm in northern Ohio not too different from the one where you now live. I was born there in 1876 (now you can figure out how old I am!). My parents—they would be your great-grandparents—had moved there before I was born from New York State, where they had been farmers. But the crops were poor in New York. Mother and Father were looking for a better life, and moving farther west seemed the way to do it.

If you think your Wisconsin farmhouse is primitive, let me tell you a little about the house where I was born. It really wasn't a house but a log cabin that my father and some of the neighbors put together when Mother and Father first moved to Ohio. I know you've read about and seen pictures of pioneer log cabins. The one I grew up in was a lot like those. It had only one room, with a big fireplace at one end and a bed with a mattress stuffed with corn shucks on the other end. That's where my parents slept. They could pull a curtain across that end of the cabin, which in a way was like having another little room.

My two little brothers (your great-uncles) and I slept upstairs in the cabin. We got there by crawling up a ladder that my father made out of oak branches. It was cozy sleeping up there, especially on a rainy night with the raindrops pounding on the roof just over our heads. It was also very dark in the cabin's loft, because there were no windows.

We didn't have real windows downstairs, either. Glass windows were scarce and too expensive for our family. My father stretched a piece of white muslin (a kind of cloth) over each window frame and then oiled the cloth to make it last longer. These makeshift windowpanes let in some light, but we couldn't see out like you can with glass windows. Our light in the cabin came from kerosene lamps, just like you have. And yes, George, we had an outdoor bathroom, too.

I'm sorry to hear that your leg is still giving you problems. But let me tell you about another person who had lots of health problems when he was your age: Theodore Roosevelt. You've probably read about him, because he became our twenty-sixth president of the United States. He didn't let being sickly get in the way of doing great things. He just held his chin up and kept going. Sometimes that's what we've all got to do.

Don't let Amos Woodward get under your skin. I think he might be jealous that you know how to do things with leather that he doesn't know how to do. And he probably enjoys teasing you because you limp—some children are like that. They like making fun of anyone who seems different. Just ignore him. It's not your fault that this Amos boy is picking on you. Something else is going on in his life. That would be my guess, anyway.

I'm so glad you are safe, and I look forward to more of your letters. I miss all of you very much.

Love,
Grandma S.

March 21, 1938
Monday

Dear Grandma,

It's the beginning of my first full week of school. I hope it goes better than last week. The only good thing about school is that I don't think I'm too far behind. We had a spelling test today, and I got a perfect score, 100 percent. I even did better than the eighth-graders. There are two of them at my school, and one is Amos Woodward, that big brown-haired kid who picks on me. He got an 85 on the test. Rachel Williams, the other eighth-grader, got a 92. Miss Harvey didn't say anything to me about my perfect score, but she did smile a little when she handed back my paper. She told us that in two weeks our school will compete with Forest Grove School at a spelling bee. I'd sure like to be on our school's spelling team.

I haven't been late for school since that one time. It's hard walking, too. With a few warmer days, the snow has been melting, and the dirt road past our farm is a river of mud. The mailman and the milkman can scarcely drive without getting stuck. The roads are better in the morning because the ruts are still frozen. This afternoon it took me nearly an hour to walk home from school, and when I got here my boots were muddy nearly to the top. Ma said I looked like I'd been jumping up and down in the muck. I said I hadn't, but I felt like a better nickname for me might be Stuck-Meyer instead of Struckmeyer. I got stuck in the mud at least three times, and one time thought for sure I'd lost my boot.

Time to do my homework.

Your grandson,
George

Dear George,

I'm so happy to receive your letters and hear about all that you are doing in Wisconsin. Did you know I went to a one-room school that was a lot like yours? Our school was made of logs, and it hadn't been built very well. In winter the cold air sifted into the room between the logs that were not chinked well. (That means the material plugging the spaces between the logs wasn't put in properly.)

Paper was scarce in those days, so we each had a slate where we worked numbers and wrote the letters of the alphabet. A slate is like a little blackboard, but small enough so that you can hold it in your hand. Of course, we also studied spelling, learned a little geography, and spent time reading and writing. It was reading and writing that I most enjoyed doing. I thought it was lots of fun to read about what other people were doing and how they did it. And I always liked writing; I still do. I am happy to hear how well you are doing in spelling. A perfect score in spelling is something special.

Do you know we played anti-I-over when I was

in school? We played it just as you described. It was so much fun! I'm glad to hear that children are still playing the old school games.

Keep writing. Your letters mean a lot to me, George. It gets pretty lonely around here without you, little Annie, and your folks nearby.

Love,
Grandma S.

March 23, 1938
Wednesday

Dear Grandma,

Did I tell you that we don't even have a radio here in the hinterlands of Wisconsin? We don't have electricity, so I didn't even ask Pa about getting a radio. But he surprised me. When I came home from school today, I saw a brand new Philco radio sitting on a little table near one of the kitchen windows. I told Pa I couldn't see how it would work without electricity, and he kind of smiled and pointed to the two big batteries that sit under the radio. Then he showed me a wire that runs from the back of the radio, outside a kitchen window, and all the way to the top of our windmill. He called it an aerial and said it will help us pull in radio stations from as far away as Chicago.

One thing I haven't complained about since we moved to Wisconsin is not being able to listen to my favorite radio programs every afternoon like I did back in Ohio. I especially like *Captain Midnight*. (Luckily I remembered to bring to bring my decoder badge along with me from Ohio, which I need to figure out the secret messages at the end of each *Captain Midnight* program.) I also like listening to *Jack Armstrong*, *Tarzan*, and *Terry and the Pirates*.

After the chores were done tonight, I snapped on the radio, gathered some paper and a pencil so I could write down the numbers the announcer reads at the end of the program (for the secret message), and sat next to our new radio. *Captain Midnight* came in just as well as it did in Ohio! What a wonderful thing a radio is.

Of course, Pa wanted a radio as badly as anybody in the family. He likes listening to the news, the farm market reports, and the weather forecasts. Ma likes her programs as well, especially *The Romance of Helen Trent*, *Ma Perkins*, and *Our Gal Sunday*. And we all listen to *Fibber McGee and Molly*. Little Annie loves it when Fibber McGee opens the closet door and everything falls out with a big clatter. We're all looking forward to Saturday night, when we'll listen to the WLS National Barn Dance show from Chicago. Here in this new place these shows feel like old friends.

Sure wish you were here so we could listen to some of them together, Grandma, like we did when we lived in Ohio.

Your grandson,
George

March 25, 1938
Friday

Dear Grandma,

I asked Pa again when I will get my puppy. At first he looked at me like he had other things on his mind. But after all, he did promise me a puppy if I'd quit complaining about having to move to Wisconsin, so he smiled and said that he sent in the order yesterday. My puppy should be here in about a week! Now I have something to look forward to. I have always wanted a dog.

Yesterday Pa bought fifty laying hens from a neighbor. He said we need fresh eggs to eat, and Ma can sell what we don't use. It was one of the first times I've seen Ma smile since we got to Wisconsin. She doesn't say much, but I don't think she likes living here. Pa keeps reminding us that we are on a Great Adventure and said again that we must keep looking at the sunny side of things. I guess he means we must keep our spirits up. But that's not easy to do. Maybe having some egg money will cheer Ma up a little.

Pa turned the chickens loose in the chicken house. They didn't seem to mind that they were in a new place at all. They went right at eating the oats that Pa had bought for them. I hope they remember that they're supposed to be laying eggs, not just eating and prowling around their new location.

Pa also bought ten Holstein milk cows yesterday. Holsteins are the ones that are black and white, but I bet you already knew that. They were delivered in a big red cattle truck, and they seemed kind of scared. I suspect everything is new for them, just like it is for me. Pa said he'll teach me how to milk and that milking will become one of my chores. Grandma, we've got to milk these cows every morning and night, every day, even on Saturdays and Sundays. When will I ever have time to work on my leather projects? This morning I was out in the barn at 5:30! The only light we have in the barn is a kerosene lantern that shines feebly, much less brightly than our lamp in the house. I pointed this out to Pa, who told me that you don't need much light to milk a cow.

The lantern hangs on a nail on the back wall, and there are shadows everywhere. It's kind of scary—I imagine all kinds of wild creatures hiding where the light doesn't reach. Pa says about all that's in the shadows is a mouse or two, and that one of our neighbors might give us a couple of barn cats to keep the mice in check.

The cows stand in a row, their necks stuck through metal and wooden bars that Pa calls stanchions. The cows can't move around much, but there is no place to go anyway, and besides, it's warm in the barn. Mornings are well below freezing here in Wisconsin, and there's still some snow on the ground.

The first time Pa showed me how to milk a cow, he told me just to watch. He sat on a little three-legged milk stool that he pulled up right under a cow, with a shiny milk pail clamped between his knees. Then he took a teat in each hand, and milk shot into the pail with a zing. He said that that all you do is squeeze and pull, squeeze and pull, and the milk will come. He made it look easy.

Don't laugh, Grandma, but the first time I tried to do this, nothing happened. Nothing. The harder I squeezed and the more I pulled, the jumpier the cow became, but still no milk came out. Pa said to just keep trying, so that's what I did. After I relaxed a little, the milk started coming—not in big squirts, but enough that I could say I was milking a cow! Tonight it went even better. But my fingers are so sore they feel like they'll drop off my hands. Pa said it will take a while for my fingers and wrists to toughen up.

Polly is one of the cows I milk. She likes to swipe me across the face with her wiry tail. That is no fun at all. Last night I got so mad at Polly when she hit me in the face with her tail that I hauled off and hit her on the rump. That was not a good thing to do. Polly jumped, tipped me over, and spilled the little milk I had in the bottom of the pail. Pa came running when he heard the noise. I told him what had happened after he helped me collect the milk stool and pail and crawl out of the straw where I'd landed. Pa was angry. He said I should never hit a cow, no matter what. He didn't need to tell me—I had already learned that lesson!

I crawled back under Polly, sat on my milk stool, stuck the milk pail between my legs, and said, "Polly, you hear me!" The big cow turned her head, her big dark eyes staring right at me. "We're in this together. You behave and don't hit me in the face with your tail, and I won't whop you on the rump with my hand."

I don't know if she understood what I was saying, but we are getting along a little better. Maybe it's because I'm learning how to milk.

The barn is filled with strange smells that I'm not used to. There's the smell of the hay that Pa feeds the cows and the smell of cow manure, of course. All of that mixes in with the smell of fresh milk, which I think is a nice, clean smell.

I'm glad I have a weekend ahead of me. I sure wish I didn't have to go to school. It's no fun. On Monday the kids are choosing up sides for ball teams, and the teacher says everybody plays, even the little kids, if they want to. I can hit a ball as well as anyone, but I can't run with my bad leg. It makes me feel awful. Whoever heard of a kid who can't run?

I wish I was back in Ohio, Grandma.

Your grandson,
George

March 26, 1938
Saturday

Dear Grandma,

When we finished the barn chores this morning, Pa asked if I'd like to go with him to a farm auction that was going on today near Willow River, which is a town about eight miles from here. I had never been to a farm auction so I didn't know what to expect. Pa said he needed some farm equipment and a team of horses. We have cows and chickens, but with the spring work coming up fast, we'll need horses to pull the machinery necessary for putting in our crops.

We weren't the only ones at the auction. Cars were lined up on both sides of the road when we got to the farm. As we walked up the road I could hear the patter of the auctioneer selling farm tools—hammers, saws, wrenches, that sort of thing. I've never heard an auctioneer before. This one sounded like a singer and a speaker combined. It was fun to listen to him and to watch the reactions of the people in the audience as he held up each item and began his spiel, trying to fetch as much money as possible.

Pa bid on a grain drill—that's what he called a machine that looks like a long box with wheels on each end and a series of disc-like things hanging from its bottom. Here's how I remember it went:

Auctioneer: "And what am I offered for this good grain drill? Do I hear twenty-five, anybody twenty-five, anybody twenty-five dollars for this good drill?"

Pa: "Twenty-five."

Auctioneer: "And who'll make it thirty? Do I hear thirty, thirty, thirty? This drill is ready to go. Just dump in some grain, hitch up your team, and you are sowing wheat or oats or whatever you want to sow. Who says thirty dollars for the drill?"

Another farmer: "Thirty."

Auctioneer: "And who'll make it thirty-five? Do I hear thirty-five? Anybody thirty-five?"

Pa: "Thirty-five."

Auctioneer: "And now forty. Who'll make it forty? Anybody? Anybody make it forty? I'm gonna sell it. Last chance. Once, twice, three times. Sold to that fellow standing in the back. And mark it cheap."

Pa won the grain drill. He also bought a four-wheeled hay wagon and a team of horses. Their names are Maud and Tony. We put the grain drill on the wagon and pulled it home behind the car. The trucker who delivered our cows was at the auction, and he told Pa he'll haul Maud and Tony to our farm. He'll get here around chore time (for country people that means around five o'clock, give or take a half hour).

Looks like we're all set to farm—at least that's what Pa said on the way home. He told me he's going to teach me how to drive the horses and how to harness them. He says I am old enough.

I don't know if I'm looking forward to driving our new team. They are big horses, Grandma. Really big! I guess they have to be big in order to pull a plow and all the other farm machinery that we have on Hillside Farm.

Your grandson,
George

March 27, 1938
Sunday

Dear Grandma,

When we got home from church this morning, Pa asked if I was ready to try my hand at driving our new team. What could I say? I mostly was worried about one of them putting its big foot down on mine.

I mentioned that to Pa, and he kind of smiled and said, "They won't do that—at least if they are like other horses I've known." That didn't do much to take away my fear.

As Pa harnessed the team, he said I should watch what he was doing, because next time I'll be doing it by myself. First he put big padded pieces of leather around each horse's neck. He called them collars. Then he gathered up a leather harness and pulled it across Maud's back and fastened it to her collar with a little strap. He buckled a couple more straps, then turned to Tony and did the same thing. Before I knew it he was finished harnessing the team—and telling me that it's easy to do. It sure doesn't look easy to me. But I guess it's one more thing I'll have to learn.

Pa led Tony out of the barn and I led Maud, fearing every minute that the big horse—did I tell you, Grandma, that both horses are brown with black tails and black manes (that's the long hair that grows on their necks)—would step on me. But she just walked along without even coming close to stepping on me.

Once outside the barn, Pa walked the horses so they stood next to each other, and then he buckled a couple of straps so they would stay that way when they walked. He handed me the driving lines, which are two long pieces of leather attached to the horses' bridles. Then he said the only way to learn how to drive a team is to do it.

So there I stood, holding the driving lines with these two gigantic horses standing a few feet in front of me. To get the horses moving, you say "giddap." Pa said, "Shake the lines a little when you say it." To stop, you say "whoa" and pull back on the lines a little. To steer, you just pull on the lines in the direction you want the horses to turn.

I must say, it all worked pretty well. Driving a team is not as difficult as I thought it would be. I marched Maud and Tony around the yard a few times, stopped, started, turned left, turned right. Nothing to it. I even forgot about my bad leg. Pa said they are a well-trained team.

Another school day tomorrow, so I better get to bed. I didn't tell Pa this, but it was kind of fun driving our new horses.

Your grandson,
George

Dear George,

You and your family are surely busy. Let's see, you now have milk cows, laying hens, and a new team of horses. Just think, here you are driving a team of horses, and you are only twelve years old. That's not easy to do. And you've learned how to milk cows by hand. That's even harder than driving horses. I'm so proud of you.

Did I tell you that I milked cows by hand when I was a little girl? It was one of my chores on the farm by the time I was ten years old. We had only three cows, and I milked them every morning and night. It was not a bad job, but our log barn wasn't very warm in winter. In summer I milked them outside when the weather was nice.

We didn't have a team of horses on the home farm like you do. My father had a team of oxen that did all the heavy work, like plowing the land and pulling a big high-wheeled cart. I didn't have much to do with them, as they were big and clumsy and moved very slowly. Their names were Fritz and Joe. They didn't wear harnesses, like your horses. All they wore was a wooden yoke that fit over their necks. When my father wanted them to turn right, he said "gee," and if he wanted them to turn left, he said "haw." There were no leather lines like you have to turn your team of horses.

Father always said Fritz and Joe were dependable. I guess that meant that they did whatever they were asked to do without complaining. Your great-grandfather never liked to hear anyone complain. He said everyone has problems, and it doesn't help to complain about them.

It's getting late, and I must go to bed. Be sure to keep writing.

Love,
Grandma S.

March 28, 1938
Monday

Dear Grandma,

I had another go-around with Amos Woodward today. It all started when we formed softball teams at morning recess. Because they are in eighth grade,

Amos and Rachel Williams are the team captains. They took turns choosing kids, until everybody was on a team except me. Amos came right out and said that a kid who can't run shouldn't be on a team. You can imagine how I felt. Miss Harvey said that I should have a chance to play if I wanted to. But Amos held his ground and said that if I couldn't run, I was not going to be on his team.

Everyone just stared at me. I didn't know what to do. I felt like running off and hiding. Finally Rachel looked at me, smiled a little, and motioned for me to be on her team. I hobbled over next to the rest of the kids she had chosen. Rachel is a tall, soft-spoken girl. She wears her black hair in braids, and she smiles easily. All the kids like her. She doesn't seem to care that I'm from the city and walk with a limp.

By the time the teams were chosen, recess was over—no time to even start a game. Miss Harvey said we'd have a ball game during noon break. She also told us that in a few weeks we're going to play against Forest Grove School, which is a few miles from here, and that we'll need lots of practice to beat them. The best players from Rachel's and Amos's teams will become the Rose Hill ball team. I sure would like to be on the school team, but I doubt I have much of a chance.

After lunch we took our places on the ball diamond. Our school doesn't even have real bases, just empty feed sacks that sit in the middle of bare spots on the ground. And none of the kids has a softball glove. You've got to have tough hands to play on this team, because the ball is always caught barehanded.

Amos's team took to the field first, and my team got ready to bat. Rachel pointed to a fourth-grader named Fred, and he stepped up to the plate to face Amos, who was pitching. Amos rolled the ball around in his hands, glared at the kid, and told him to look out or he might hit him in the head.

I could see fear in the kid's face as he held the bat. He swung wildly at three pitches and was out. Same with the next two batters. Then it was our turn to take the field. Rachel put me in right field. I hoped no balls would come my way, and none did.

Amos's team got a couple of runs before they were out and it was our turn to bat again. Rachel pointed to me and said I should bat first this inning. I grabbed the bat, held it like I learned to do in Ohio, took a couple of practice swings, and stood up to home plate (which is just a flat piece of wood from the woodshed). I thought to myself, this guy doesn't scare me with his glares and threats. Deep inside though, I'm scared of Amos. He's bigger than I am and can throw harder than any other kid in school.

The first pitch sailed past my nose, missing me by only a couple inches. I tried not to let Amos know that it bothered me, but it did. I wasn't sure I could move fast enough if he decided to throw a ball at my head.

The next pitch flew right across the plate. I swung, but I caught only a piece of it. Even so, the ball flew over the second baseman's head and fell in centerfield. I started out for first base, forgetting about my bad leg for a minute. I hadn't taken three steps when I fell in a heap, giving the second baseman plenty of time to throw me out. I got up and limped off the field.

Grandma, everyone laughed at me. Amos pointed his long finger at me and said, "See why you're not on my team? You're no good. You can't even make it to first base, even when you get a lucky hit."

I was afraid that Rachel would toss me off the team, but she didn't say anything, and the game went on. I stood off to the side. Nobody wanted to talk to me. About ten minutes before the end of noon break, the game was tied 4 to 4, and it was my team's turn to bat. Rachel was up first, and she hit a high ball that the center fielder caught. The next player struck out. Rachel motioned at me to step up and bat.

All I could think to say was, "You mean me?"

"Yes, you. We need a hit."

I grabbed the bat and limped up to the plate. My leg was throbbing.

When I took my place at home plate, Amos looked right at me and said, "Well, if it isn't Limpy Struckmeyer. Gonna fall down on the way to first base again? Or are you gonna stand there and let me hit you in the head?" I wish our teacher had been outside to hear him. Maybe she would have told him to shut his mouth.

I felt like dropping the bat and running into the schoolhouse. But I stood my ground, something Pa has drummed into me. He always says that when you face a tough situation, you should look it right in the eye. And that's what I did. It helped that Rachel stood up for me and told Amos to stop teasing me. Sometimes Amos listens to Rachel.

Amos whistled a fastball past me that I should have let go, but I took a mighty swing at it, almost falling down in the process. I must have twisted my leg, and now it hurts even to stand on it, let alone walk.

The next pitch was fast and right across the plate. I had my eye on the dirty gray softball from the moment it left Amos's hand, and I was ready. I knew I hit the ball squarely the minute my bat made contact. Rather than start for first base, I watched the ball go higher, higher until it flew over the schoolyard fence and landed in the middle of the dirt road that runs past our school.

Can you believe it, Grandma? I hit a home run. I still had to make my way around the bases, and I did, hobbling to first, limping on to second, then on to third, and making it home just in time. Our team won, and I had made the difference with my home run. This was the best I have felt since moving to Wisconsin. But then Amos came up to me, looked me right in the eye, and told me that I'll never hit another home run and he'll make sure of it. Then he said, "No limpy city kid is gonna make fun of me."

I didn't say anything as I hobbled away. Some of my teammates walked with me to the schoolhouse. A couple of the kids even patted me on the back.

Grandma, I think Amos hates me more than ever. I don't know what to do. When I told Pa about Amos, all he said was that I should behave myself and stay out of trouble. But he also says I should stand up for what's right. What do you think I should do?

Love,
George

Dear George,

It's too bad you are still having problems with Amos Woodward. I've been thinking about what you could do to make things better. One thing you might try when he says something mean is to stare straight at him and then walk away. If he thinks what he is saying doesn't bother you (even though I know it really does), he might leave you alone.

You could also try looking him in right in the eye and saying "Stop it." Don't raise your voice, and try not to get angry. Let him believe that you are in control. Then turn and walk away.

I know that sometimes you feel like yelling at Amos. That's what he wants you do. Surprise him by not doing it. And no matter what you might hear some people say, don't hit him. Not only will he have won the battle before it even starts because he got you to lose your temper, but one or both of you will get hurt. That's never a good thing, no matter what.

Above all, George, don't let him make you feel bad. I know that can be hard, but even though you might limp a little, think about all the good things you can do. You can do really fine leather work. And you are becoming a fine writer as well. You described your softball game so well, I felt as if I was right there watching it. You should be proud of who you are. Remember what I said about President Theodore Roosevelt: he had some tough times when he was a boy, and look at what he accomplished.

Rachel Williams is surely on your side. I'll bet several of the other kids are, too. They might be keeping quiet because they are afraid of Amos.

Let me know if any of these ideas work. I know it's no fun when someone keeps picking on you.

Much love,
Grandma S.

April 1, 1938
Friday

Dear Grandma

When Pa came in for breakfast after doing the morning chores, he told Ma in a serious voice, "Emily, something awful has happened in the chicken house." He said he thought a fox must have broken in last night, and she'd better have a look for herself. Ma was really upset, because she knows that a fox will steal any number of chickens. She pulled on her chore jacket, tied a scarf over her head, and hurried out to the chicken house.

In a few minutes she was back in the kitchen with a strange look on her face. She said she had counted her chickens, and all fifty were there. Pa looked serious at first, but then he smiled and blurted out, "April fool!" It is April first, and Pa had pulled a good one on Ma—except she didn't take it as a joke. Ma was really mad, and she told Pa he could fix his own breakfast and that would be an April fool joke on him.

Pa said something about it being only a joke, but Ma didn't want to hear anything about it. She was fuming. She said nobody should make jokes about her chickens, because without the eggs there would be no grocery money and no money for Christmas presents, either.

Pa said he was sorry, but Ma said sorry wasn't good enough. I don't think the two of them talked to each other all day. So much for April Fool's Day.

Your grandson,
George

April 4, 1938
Monday

Dear Grandma,

Your letter came today. Thank you for writing. I hope you're right that if I don't talk back to Amos and try to ignore him, he'll quit picking on me. I've been trying to figure out why he hates me. All I did was hit a home run so his team lost. Since that day, Amos just snarls at me, like a mean dog that wants to bite. What do you do with a mean dog? I try to stay out of his way, but our school is too small for that.

Rachel Williams is a good friend. She looks at what I can do instead of what I can't do. I'm glad she

gave me a chance to play softball. We've been playing every day, but I don't get to play much, except to
hit once in a while. My hitting has never been like it
was that first day, maybe because I'm afraid of Amos
and can't concentrate. My running is as bad as ever.
Whenever I try, I fall down. I feel terrible about that.

Grandma, is there a way for me to move back to
Ohio? I haven't mentioned this to Pa and Ma, but I
think about it all the time. If I left this terrible school
and moved away from this farm with all the chores,
my life would be so much better. What do you think,
Grandma?

Love,
George

April 9, 1938
Saturday

Dear Grandma,

Right after we finished breakfast this morning, our
telephone rang. The telephone hangs on the wall in
the kitchen, and Ma always answers it when it rings
our ring, which isn't very often. We are on a party
line, which means that several people in our neighborhood are connected to the same telephone line.
The only way you know when to answer the telephone is when you hear your own special ring. Ours
is one long ring and three short rings. We can ring

each other on our party line, but when we want to talk to people who aren't on our party line, we have to ring up central, which is the telephone office in Link Lake. All calls from one party line to another go through central.

Ma told Pa the call was for him. As he listened to whoever was on the other end, a big grin spread across his face. Then he said thank you, hung up the receiver, and asked if I would like to ride into town with him. He wouldn't say who had called, but he sure was grinning. He told me to pull on my jacket and meet him at the car.

I started to ask Pa what all the hurry was about, but he was all wrapped up in his thoughts and told me I'd know soon enough. When we got to Link Lake, he pulled into the little parking lot at the train depot, which is just outside of the village. Now I was really confused. Why were we stopping here? We never stop at the Link Lake Depot when we go to Link Lake. The depot is a little one-story building that stands next to the railroad tracks that run through town. At each end of the building is a large sign that reads "Link Lake." The depot is where the trains stop that travel east and west through Link Lake.

I asked Pa why we were stopping at the train depot, and this time he said that I'd find out in a few minutes. Inside the little building, Pa walked up to a man behind a counter. He told the man his name and introduced me. The fellow is called the depot agent. He came out from behind the counter, shook both our hands, and said his name is Floyd Johnson. Then he said he had something special for us, and he motioned for us to follow him.

We walked across the waiting room, past a bunch of empty chairs and a big woodstove. Mr. Johnson stopped at a small wooden crate sitting on the floor near the stove. The crate was maybe three feet square, with spaces between the boards on the sides. "Here's your order, Mr. Struckmeyer," the depot agent said to Pa. "Came on the morning train from Fond du Lac." He released a latch and pulled open the door on one end of the crate. Pa said I should look inside. I got down on my knees and came face to face with a furry little brown puppy with a long nose and big brown eyes!

I asked Pa, "Is this my puppy?"

"It sure is," Pa replied. "Cute little fellow, isn't he?" He told me to let the pup sniff my hand. When I reached in my hand, the puppy licked it. I couldn't help but laugh.

Pa told me to take the puppy out of the box so we all could have a look at him. I picked up the pup, and this time he licked my face. Pa said that the kennel owner wrote him that the puppy is a collie, and he was born on February 2. He weighs about fifteen pounds now, and he'll grow to weigh as much as seventy-five pounds. The depot agent said this puppy is just about the finest one he's ever seen.

I put the puppy back in the crate, and Pa helped me put the crate on the back seat of our car. I kept looking back at him all the way home. I felt about as happy as I've been in a long time, Grandma. Then Pa asked what I planned to name him. I hadn't even thought about whether the little collie pup had a name or if I'd get to name him. But a name quickly came to mind. I told Pa I'd like to name him Depot, because that's where I first saw him. Pa said the name sounds a little unusual, but if it's the name I want, then Depot shall be his name.

Back at home I carried the crate into the kitchen and set it down in front of the kitchen stove where Ma was working. Ma smiled when she saw the puppy in the crate. I guess she knew how much I had wanted one.

Little Annie was sitting on a stool next to the stove, watching Ma cook. She hopped off the stool and stood watching as I leaned over, opened the door on the crate, and took out my furry puppy. I told them, "His name is Depot."

Annie started giggling and asked if she could pet him. I held the puppy out for her. Depot licked her face, which made Annie giggle even more.

Ma said Depot is a cute puppy. Then she reminded me that it will be my job to take care of him, to make sure he gets something to eat and drink and that he stays out of trouble. She went on for a bit about how puppies are known to get into all sorts of trouble. I told her I'll watch him real good. And I will.

This was just about the best day I've ever had, Grandma. You would really like Depot. He's just the nicest little puppy.

Your grandson,
George

April 10, 1938
Sunday

Dear Grandma,

Wouldn't you know it? I've had Depot for only one day, and already both he and I are in trouble. I forgot to fasten the latch on his crate when I went to bed last night. During the night he got out and roamed around the kitchen. He found a basket of Ma's newly washed clothes, and did he have fun! He scattered shirts and underwear all over the place, from one end of the kitchen to the other. Was Ma ever mad. She said she'll have to wash the clothes all over again and that it was my fault for not latching Depot's crate.

Grandma, I'm in trouble with Ma, and I deserve it, especially after I promised her that this sort of thing wouldn't happen. I thought Pa would be after me, too, for not latching the crate properly, but he didn't say anything. In fact, I caught him smiling a little when he saw what Depot had done to the clothes.

Annie thought Depot was just having a little fun, and she said so. That sure didn't help matters. Ma blurted out that my puppy better learn to have fun with something besides her clean clothes.

I've got to remember to latch that crate at night.

Something else happened today that I must tell you about. The railroad tracks are only about a half mile from our farm, and a train goes by in the morning and in the afternoon—I can hear the engineer blowing the steam engine's whistle when the train crosses over country roads. Pa says the train runs from Fond du Lac to Marshfield, where it connects to other train lines.

Well, this afternoon, while I was doing homework at the kitchen table, there came a knock on the door. I thought it was one of our neighbors coming calling—we haven't met all of them yet, so I figured someone was stopping by to say hello. It didn't occur to me that I hadn't heard a car drive in.

I pulled open the door, and there stood the skinniest, saddest looking man I've ever seen. His clothes were dirty and torn. His shoes looked about worn out, and he wore a dirty gray hat, which he took off when I opened the door. For a minute I didn't know what to say, but then I did what Pa always says to do when someone knocks on the door: I invited him in.

By now Pa, Ma, and Annie had come into the kitchen. We all stood there looking at this forlorn man, who was clearly down on his luck.

In a near whisper, the man said he hadn't eaten since yesterday and asked if we had a spare piece of bread. Right away Ma said that she would make him a sandwich.

"I'll work for it," the man said. "I'm still strong. I can split some wood for you. Do whatever work needs doing."

Pa told him he didn't have to work for it and that Sunday is a day of rest. He invited the man to have a seat and tell us a little bit about his situation. I think Pa figured from the fellow's appearance that he'd been caught up in the Depression, had probably lost his job, and was riding the rails looking for whatever work he could find and begging for food. And Pa was right. The fellow had come from Chicago. He was laid off from his job more than six months ago and is working his way north riding the freight trains and trying to find work. He said his name is George, just like mine.

He finished off the sandwich Ma put in front of him and drank a big glass of milk. Ma asked him if he wanted more, and he quietly said that another sandwich would be wonderful.

Before he left, Ma packed some bread and sausage in a bag. I saw her tuck in a few sugar cookies, too. The man stood at the door and thanked us again and again, and I think he had tears in his eyes. And then he was gone. I watched him walk slowly down our country road until he was out of sight.

Pa shook his head and said that the Depression is a terrible thing. "That was a good man who sat at our table," Pa said. "I wonder what will happen to him?"

Pa didn't have to remind us that we moved to Wisconsin because he lost his job in Ohio. We sure are a lot better off than this poor guy, who is sneaking rides on trains and spending a lot of time walking along country roads, begging for something to eat.

Your grandson,
George

Dear George,

What fun you must be having with a new puppy! Depot is a great name, and it fits him, too. You are a very clever fellow to come up with a name like that. In one of your earlier letters you seemed sad about living in Wisconsin. With your new little puppy as part of your family, things will surely look better for you.

I know you and your little sister will have lots of fun with Depot, but remember that puppies are just like any other baby: you've got to look after them. Puppies especially like to chew on things, it's their nature. And sometimes they chew on things they shouldn't, like one of your Pa's shoes.

Puppies also can get into trouble with other animals, especially wild animals. They don't know any better. Puppies are really curious. When I was a little girl, we had a puppy that waddled off and got in the chicken yard. I heard the little guy yipping after a big red rooster pecked him on the nose. He never bothered that old rooster again. I felt bad for the puppy, but it was kind of funny, too. Nothing tangled with our red rooster. He was king of the chicken yard.

Love,
Grandma S.

April 11, 1938
Monday

Dear Grandma,

When I got home from school today, Pa asked me to drive the team over to the Williams farm and pick up ten sacks of seed oats. The Williams family—and my schoolmate Rachel—live about a mile north of our farm. You'll remember that Rachel picked me to be on her softball team a few weeks ago.

I have been practicing driving the team, and I was proud that Pa wanted me to drive them over to the neighbors' place all by myself. I've also learned how to harness the team by myself; harnessing a horse is a lot more complicated than it looks.

Soon I was seated on the wagon and on my way down our driveway with the team walking out front with their heads high. I waved to Pa and then returned to keeping a tight grip on the driving reins. Maud and Tony are fast walkers. In a few minutes we were out of sight of our farm. The wagon's steel wheels bounced along the gravel road, making interesting sounds as they ran over stones. The weathered gray wagon box rattled and shook, but I was quite comfortable on my driving seat with springs. I relaxed a little and let the team have their heads as they stepped off down the road.

Mr. Williams saw me coming and motioned for me to drive up to the granary door, which I did. I said "whoa" to Maud and Tony, and they stopped as nice as you please. I crawled off the wagon seat and tied the team to a post by the granary door. Pa has told me never to leave the team without tying them, because you never know when something might scare them and they'll run off. I had never seen anything scare Maud and Tony, but I tied them to the post anyway and helped Mr. Williams drag the sacks of seed oats onto the wagon.

Mr. Williams asked if Pa is about ready to sow

oats. I told him that we'll be putting the seed in the ground just as soon as Pa works up the oat field—which means plowing, discing, and smoothing the field. One thing I'm learning, Grandma, is a new language. Maybe because you grew up on a farm you already knew "work up," but it is new to me.

When we were just about finished loading the sacks of seed oats, Rachel came from around the barn carrying something furry in her arms. It didn't look like a barn cat. She said hi and asked if I'd like to meet Gregory, her pet raccoon. I'd never seen a pet raccoon before. She told me she found it when it was a baby. Something had happened to its mother, and it was all on its own.

Grandma, I wish you could see Gregory. He is about the cutest animal you'd ever want to look at. He's got big bright eyes, a nose like a puppy dog's, and two cute little ears that stand straight up. And do you know what? He has a black mask that makes him look like a furry little outlaw. Rachel says he knows all kinds of tricks, like begging for food and holding his paws together like he is praying.

I wished I had more time to spend with Rachel and Gregory, but I knew that Pa was waiting for me at home, so I untied the team and headed back down the road toward home. With the ten sacks of oats on the wagon, Maud and Tony walked a little slower. It was a pleasant time to be on the road. I could smell the soil in the fields that had already been plowed. I even saw a wedge of wild geese winging north. Grandma, what a wonderful sound they make, honking as they fly. I watched the great Vs change as new geese took up the job of leading the flock.

Then I saw something in the underbrush alongside the road up ahead of the team. Suddenly a fox jumped out in the road, its big bushy tail sticking straight out behind it. The horses saw the fox at the same time I did. Tony snorted and reared on his hind legs, and then Maud did. Wow—it was scary seeing the team on their hind legs pawing the air and snorting like everything!

I pulled on the lines and yelled "whoa" at the top of my lungs. But it did no good. The team took off on a gallop toward home. I yanked on the lines as hard as I could, but there was no stopping them. I kept yelling "whoa, whoa," but they didn't slow one bit. Then we got to a little turn in the road, and that's where it happened. The wagon flipped over on its side, throwing me into the neighbor's plowed field and spilling the seed oats in the ditch.

When the wagon tipped, Maud and Tony finally stopped. I got up from the muddy field and hobbled over to the wagon. I was muddy from one end to the other, but I wasn't hurt. Maud and Tony seemed all right, too, although they were breathing pretty hard. Pa had been watching me driving down the road, and he came running when he saw what happened. He grabbed the team by their bridles and calmed them down. Then he unhitched the team from the overturned wagon and said that we'd need some help in righting it, and that'd we'd have to shovel up as many of the seed oats as we could. I thought he was going to give me the dickens, but he didn't. He just asked if I was hurt and what happened. I told him about the fox running in front of the horses.

He said it doesn't take much to spook a team. I

know one thing, Grandma, I'll never let the lines rest in my lap again. I didn't tell Pa that I wasn't holding the lines tight when the fox jumped in front of the horses.

Your grandson,
George

Dear George,

Depot appears to be a normal little puppy, getting into all kind of things he shouldn't. If you want to stay on your Ma's good side, you'll need to do a better job of watching after him. I'm sure you already know that.

I'm glad your Ma gave some food to the man who stopped by your house. This Depression is a terrible thing, indeed, and it just keeps hanging on, month after month, year after year. I know it's tough for farmers like your Pa who have to contend with low prices. But I think it's even worse in the big cities, like here in Cleveland. Twenty-five percent of our people who want to work do not have jobs. Can you imagine that? One-fourth of the people have no income, just like the fellow who stopped by your house asking for something to eat. Most of these men who are on the road have families, too. It's just terrible. I know you don't have it easy living on a farm, but at least you and your family have a roof over your heads and plenty to eat.

I spend some of my time volunteering at a soup kitchen in downtown Cleveland. A soup kitchen is a place where people can get a free meal. You should see the line of people waiting at noon each day. Every week the line seems to grow longer. You can tell by people's clothes, all faded and patched, that they have no money. About all we're able to give them at the soup kitchen is a slice of bread and a bowl of hot soup, sometimes with a little meat in it.

I'm lucky to have a little money from your grandfather's savings. It's enough so I have food to eat. So many people have nothing—no money for food, no money for clothes. I just don't know where it's all going to end. I'm trying to stay cheerful about it all. Your letters help me. Keep them coming. After a few hours of work at the soup kitchen, I need all the cheering up I can get.

Much love,
Grandma S.

April 15, 1938
Friday

Dear Grandma,

Good news, Grandma: Miss Harvey selected me for the spelling team! Rachel Williams and Amos Woodward are the other two members. Amos didn't want me on the team, so he said the spelling team shouldn't have any new students on it. Because I have attended Rose Hill for only a few weeks, I shouldn't be eligible, he said. Miss Harvey didn't see it that way and shushed Amos when he complained.

I felt like holding up my hand and telling Miss Harvey that Amos shouldn't be on the team because he doesn't spell all that well, but I thought better of it. Pa always says that there are times when it's best to keep your mouth shut. I figured this was one of those times.

We've been practicing every afternoon. We started out with easy words like "dessert" and "antique." Miss Harvey keeps making them harder, and we three compete against each other. The first day Rachel won, and the second day I won. So far Amos hasn't won any of the practice matches. He isn't too happy about it, either.

Miss Harvey came up with the word "epistemology" one day. I asked if it really is a word. She smiled and said it surely is, and that it means the study of knowledge. None of us could even pronounce the word, so Miss Harvey wrote on the board: epis-te-mol-o-gy. Amos said it's a dumb word and asked why we should practice a word that will never be in a spelling bee. Miss Harvey said you can never be too sure about that, so we'd best learn how to both pronounce it and spell it.

Another word we have practiced is "chrysanthemum." Now I know why most people say "mum" when they talk about this flower. "Chrysanthemum" is a mouthful. Miss Harvey wrote the syllables on the blackboard: chry-san-the-mum.

Practicing for a spelling bee is kind of fun, except for having Amos on the team. He hates me, Grandma.

Your grandson,
George

Dear George,

It's another rainy, dreary day in Ohio. All the people out of work here in Cleveland don't help matters, either. One bright spot for me is receiving your letters and hearing all about what you are doing.

Congratulations on being selected for your school's spelling team! Good luck at the upcoming spelling bee with the neighboring school. Spelling bees are lots of fun.

You are lucky you didn't get hurt when the horses ran away when a fox frightened them. That must have been a scary experience for you. I know it would have been for me. Whatever work you are doing, especially if it involves animals, you must never let your guard down. Of course, you know that now without me having to point it out to you.

Keep practicing your spelling. I'm sure you know that being a good speller will help you become an even better writer. I'm rooting for you, and I can't wait to hear how the spelling bee turns out. And keep trying to ignore Amos Woodward.

Love,
Grandma S.

April 16, 1938
Saturday

Dear Grandma,

Today Pa hitched Maud and Tony to the grain drill. (Remember that Pa won the grain drill at an auction last month? It has two big iron wheels and discs that cut little trenches in the soil where it places the seed oats.) Then he sowed the big field just south of the barn with seed oats. I was afraid that because I had spilled some of our seed oats when the team ran away, Pa wouldn't have enough. But he did. With the seed oats in the ground, Pa says that we now must wait for the crop to come up. But we don't really sit around and watch the field as you might think; we are always doing other things, like fixing fence. Winter snows always knock down fence posts and wire, and we can't turn the cows out to pasture until the fences are in good shape.

Pa says you never know what you might find in a fencerow. Most of our fencerows are piled with rocks that were hauled off the fields by previous farmers on this land. These rock piles make great dens for foxes and homes for cottontail rabbits. Pa said he saw a jackrabbit near one of the fencerows where he sowed oats. Jackrabbits are about twice as big as cottontail rabbits, which are more common around here. During the winter Pa says jackrabbits turn all white, except for the tips of their ears, so they are better camouflaged in the snow. In the spring, their coat turns brown again. I'd sure like to see one of those big rabbits.

Before Pa could sow the field to oats, we had to haul off the stones. New stones rise to the surface every year. We have to get them out of the field, because if you strike a stone with a piece of farm machinery, there is a good chance you will break the machine. Pa says the stones came to our farm all the way from Canada. The great glacier brought the stones to Wisconsin thousands of years ago.

Picking stones is hard, dirty work, Grandma. We hitched Maud and Tony to the stone boat, which really isn't a boat at all. It is made from several boards that are bent up in the front and bolted together. Pa says that white oak makes the best stone boat because it's tough and doesn't wear out. Our stone boat is about eight feet long and four feet wide. It looks like a sled without runners.

It's a real trick to ride standing up on a stone boat. There is nothing to hold on to as the boat glides along the plowed ground. Sometimes when the boat hits a bump, I fly off and land in the newly plowed ground, which is as soft as a feather bed, so I don't get hurt, only dirty. After we pick stones, I am dust and dirt from the top of my straw hat to the tips of my shoes.

Pa showed me a trick for keeping my balance while I bounce across our plowed fields in the stone boat. He said I should bend my knees and lean forward a little. I tried doing that, and it helped. Most of the time I'm able to keep standing, but my bad leg doesn't help matters. It doesn't bend as easily as my good leg.

Do you know what, Grandma? We picked fifteen stone boat loads of field stones in one day. Can you imagine that?

Time to do some homework and be off to bed. I am really tired.

Your grandson,
George

April 17, 1938
Sunday

Dear Grandma,

We just got home from Easter services at church. I don't think I told you that we go to a Norwegian church on the shores of a little lake. Although the people who go to church there are mostly Norwegians, the service is in English. Pa said that if we'd been going to this church ten or fifteen years ago, the service would have been in Norwegian. Ma said she would be happier if we could go to a German church, because we are German, but it sure doesn't make any difference to me. We always sit three rows from the front, near a window. Since it has gotten warmer, the windows usually are open a little, and I can look out at the lake. I saw a fish jump this morning. I told Pa about it when we got home, and he said it was probably a black bass. He said we should take our fishing poles over there sometime and see if we can catch it. He also told me not to mention seeing the fish to Ma, because she'll say I should be paying attention to what the preacher has to say and not be gawking out the window.

　　I don't think little Annie cares much for church, either. I think she would rather be digging in the dirt lot out in front of the church, but she sits next to Ma, fidgeting and squirming until Ma gives her one of her looks, which is the kind of stare that will sour milk. When it comes to church, you don't disagree with Ma.

We had a big Easter dinner, and then Ma gave us the little packages you sent for Annie and me. Thank you so much for the chocolate rabbit—it's the only Easter present I got. Thanks for your letter, too.

Your grandson,
George

April 18, 1938
Monday

Dear Grandma,

Yesterday I met Grandma Woodward. She lives only a half mile from our farm and is Amos Woodward's grandmother. On my way to school I walk past her neat farmstead with its red barn, a few outbuildings, and a little white house with a porch across the front. Pa told me she doesn't have a car and doesn't get out much.

Pa had offered to plow her garden, and that's what we did yesterday after we got home from church and finished dinner. We loaded the walking plow onto the stone boat, hitched it up behind the team, and drove them the short distance down the road to Grandma Woodward's place.

Grandma, I think you would like Grandma

Woodward. She reminds me so much of you. She is little—I'm taller than she is—and has white hair fashioned in some kind of knot on the back of her head. Ma says you call that a bun. (I thought buns were for eating, but I didn't question it.) She has a thin face and blue eyes and is always smiling. Pa says she is "as skinny as a split rail fence." And she is so nice. While Pa was plowing her garden, she brought out some white sugar cookies for me, and I sat with her on the porch, talking.

She likes to talk, Grandma, just like you, and she also listens. She wanted to know how I am doing in school, and I told her about the upcoming spelling bee. I got a little nervous when she asked if I know Amos. I said I do, but I didn't tell her how Amos picks on me. She said she worries about Amos. I didn't know what to say, but I wondered what she meant.

Grandma Woodward asked me about my leg, and I told her the story. She asked me what I like to do, and I said I like reading, writing, and making leather projects. She said she'd like to see some of the leather work I've done and asked me to stop by again sometime soon. She is such a nice lady.

Well, it's time to go to sleep, so I must quit writing.

Your grandson,
George

April 23, 1938
Saturday

Dear Grandma,

Last night we had our spelling bee at school. Everyone from the community was invited, and I think
most of them came, along with lots of folks from the
Forest Grove School District. Forest Grove School is
only a couple hills and three bends in the road away.

With all our practicing, our team thought we
could spell just about any word that came along.
Miss Harvey set the starting time for eight o'clock
so everyone would have time to finish their evening
chores. When Pa, Ma, Annie, and I got there at
seven-thirty, cars were already lined up on both sides
of the road. Pa said it looked like a Christmas program crowd, but I've never been to a school Christmas program, so I don't know what that's like. A lot
of parents were there, and I spotted Grandma Woodward sitting close to the front of the room.

When Miss Harvey saw me, she took my arm
and introduced me to the spelling team from Forest
Grove School: two girls, Violet and Joyce, and a boy
named Herman.

Grandma, I thought the kids in our school were
poor, but you should have seen these kids. Herman's
flannel shirt was so faded it didn't have any color at
all. His worn-out bib overalls came halfway up to
his knees because they were too small for him. I tried
not to smile when I saw this big, tall, gawky looking
kid with the high-water pants—that's what Pa calls
pants that are too short. (He means they're so short
they'll stay dry even in a flood.) The girls' clothes

weren't any better. Their dresses had been washed so many times that they had no color at all. Well, I took one look at this threesome and figured our team wouldn't have much trouble at this spelling bee. It looked to me like these kids have trouble just finding enough to eat, and they surely must not have time to practice for a spelling bee.

At eight Miss Harvey stood up and welcomed everyone to our school. She spoke for a while about how important it is to know how to spell. I was so nervous I don't remember what else she said. Then she introduced Miss Johnson, a plump woman with black hair and big arms. Miss Harvey said Miss Johnson was from the county superintendent of school's office and was going to read the words to be spelled. Miss Johnson wore a dress all plastered with big red flowers. She looked like something was paining her; maybe that flowered dress was too tight.

Miss Harvey introduced the Forest Grove School spelling team and their teacher, Miss Zilinski. Finally she introduced Amos, Rachel, and me. Grandma, my stomach was churning. I knew this team was no competition for us, but I was still scared. What frightened me most was standing up in front of so many people—every seat in the school was taken. Men were standing all around the woodstove in back and clear out the entryway doors.

Our guests got the first chance to spell. Miss Johnson pulled down on her tight dress, cleared her throat, and, in a voice that sounded like she was sitting on a tack, said the first word: "library."

Violet from Forest Grove School stood up, and in a thin voice I could scarcely hear, spelled, "l-i-b-r-a-r-y." Miss Johnson asked her to repeat with a louder voice. Poor Violet was so nervous. I saw her hands shaking.

"Correct," Miss Johnson said after she heard the spelling a second time. Compared to Violet, Miss Johnson's voice seemed to hit the ceiling and bounce all around the room.

Now it was our team's turn, and Amos was first.

"Whistle," Miss Johnson said.

"W-i-s-t-le," spelled Amos. Whistle hadn't been one of our practice words, and Amos spelled it like it sounds.

"Incorrect," said Miss Johnson.

Amos stammered, "But, but . . . ," but Miss Johnson told him to sit down.

Amos was steaming. His face was as red as a male cardinal, and he was pounding a fist against his head.

Joyce from Forest Grove School got "whistle" right without even stopping to think. I began wondering if this team was going to be the pushover that I had thought.

After a few more rounds, just two of us remained unbeaten, Joyce from Forest Grove School and me. The next word was "liaison." I spelled it l-a-y-s-o-n, but Miss Johnson said that was wrong. The only chance our team had was if Joyce missed it, too. She stood up, fidgeted a little, and spelled, "l-i-a-s-i-o-n."

"Incorrect," said Miss Johnson. Then she told us the correct spelling: "L-i-a-i-s-o-n."

Since our teams were tied, Miss Johnson said we would do one more round of spelling to see if there would be a winner. It was Joyce's turn to go first.

The word was "chalice." Miss Johnson pronounced it twice and even gave its definition: "a holy cup used in church services." I have never heard the word before, and I tried to think how I would spell it in case Joyce missed.

Joyce really took her time spelling the word. "C-h . . ." She took a deep breath and finished, "a-l-i-c-e."

"Now it's your turn, young man," Miss Johnson told me. I spelled, "s-h-a-l-l-i-c-e." When I finished, I glanced at Miss Harvey, and from the look on her face I knew I got it wrong.

"Forest Grove School wins the spelling bee!" Miss Johnson announced in her big voice, her dress starting to creep up above her knees again. "Congratulations to the winners and to the losers, too. I think we've all learned something about spelling this evening."

That was it. We lost. On the way to the car, I saw Amos Woodward's pa yelling at him and cuffing him on the head. Then I heard Grandma Woodward telling Amos that he had tried and that she was proud of him. She spotted me and told me what a good job I had done, too. But I still went home feeling terrible.

Ma said I had done well just by being on the team. But I learned more than how to spell "chalice." Those poorly dressed kids from Forest Grove School sure know how to spell.

Your grandson,
George

P.S. I'm so wrapped up in spelling that I had to look at my name twice to see if I spelled it right!

Dear George,

How I enjoyed your long letter of last Saturday! Thank you for sharing with me all the details of the spelling bee. I'm sure you learned a lot from it. Those were some very difficult words you had to spell.

I know you've thought a lot about this, but when you meet people like the students from the other school who are obviously very poor, it's easy to make judgments about them. I'll bet you've heard the saying, "You can't judge a book by its cover." There is certainly some truth to it, especially when it comes to people, and I suspect especially when it comes to poor people.

I'm learning a lot about poor people these days when I volunteer at the soup kitchen. Some of the smartest people I've ever met are now standing in lines waiting to get a bowl of soup and a slice of bread. It's terrible what this Depression is doing to people. So many good people have been made to feel worthless.

You mentioned Amos and how his father cuffed him on the head after your team lost the spelling bee. Do you suppose that the way Amos's father treats him is one of the reasons that Amos acts like he does? It's something to think about.

Keep the letters coming.

Much love,
Grandma S.

April 30, 1938
Saturday

Dear Grandma,

Sorry I haven't written, but we have been busy with spring planting and fixing fence so we can turn the cows out on pasture, at least on the warm days.

The grass is "greening up," as people around here say. In church last Sunday, I heard frogs calling in the nearby lake. Pa calls them spring peepers. I even heard a red-winged blackbird—saw it, too—perched on a cattail. Red-winged blackbirds look like someone fastened a piece of red cloth to each wing. Pa told me that only the males have red on their wings; the females are entirely brownish black. I asked him why women and girls always wear colorful dresses and skirts, and men and boys look plain and drab. He smiled and said he guessed people are the opposite of birds. Another thing for me to ponder, I guess.

Remember Polly? She's the cow that tipped me over when I was learning how to milk. Polly had been dry for several weeks—that means she was getting ready to have a calf, and I wasn't milking her. She finally had her calf a couple days ago, a beautiful little heifer with a nearly all-white face and big dark eyes. She was standing up nursing inside of an hour. Pa said I should pick out a name for the little calf, and I decided on Jane.

Polly seemed okay after the calf was born—she

was standing up, eating hay, and letting Jane nurse—but Pa says things aren't right with Polly and that we should watch her closely for a few days. I told Pa I'll keep an eye on her, but I don't really know what I'm looking for.

Every time I watch Jane nursing, I have to smile, because the little calf seems so eager to eat. She pushes her muzzle into Jane's udder and sucks like everything. While the calf nurses, her tail—white with a black tip—swings back and forth. It is something to see, Grandma.

Yesterday we took Jane away from Polly and put the little calf in a pen. I am milking Polly again. Pa said she gives a lot more milk than Jane can drink, and we need the money from the milk we sell.

It is my job to teach Jane to drink from a pail. What a project! Pa taught me to straddle the calf, which means I put a leg on each side of her neck. Then I hold the pail of milk in one hand and gently push the calf's head into the pail with the other hand while at the same time letting the calf suck on my fingers. That little calf has a tongue that feels just like sandpaper.

Once Jane tasted the milk, she gave a great push with her head. She almost spilled the pail, and she splashed milk all over me. Pa stood there laughing. He told me to keep trying—sometimes it takes several tries before a calf learns how to drink from a pail.

By about the third time, Jane figured out that she has to keep her muzzle in the pail to drink.

Polly still isn't doing well, and Pa is worried. She didn't give near as much milk today as she did yesterday, and she isn't eating much. I surely hope Polly isn't getting sick.

I haven't told you about Depot lately. Is he ever growing! He's outside a lot now, and whenever I'm home we are together. He even comes into the barn when we're doing chores. Just the other night, after I had poured some milk in the cat dish and the barn cats had gathered, Depot decided he wanted a drink of milk, too. Big mistake for Depot. He pushed his way up to the cat dish, and a barn cat scratched him on the nose. He yipped and ran toward me where I was milking a cow. I think he's learned not to mess with the barn cats.

We got the barn cats from our neighbor, Mr. Williams. He had more than he needed and gave us four. These cats aren't pets, though—far from it. According to Pa, barns cats have one purpose, and that is to catch mice around the barn.

Has spring come to Ohio? We are all happy to be through with winter here in Wisconsin. At least, I think we are through with it.

Your grandson,
George

May 2, 1938
Monday

Dear Grandma,

When I got out to the barn this morning, Polly looked like she was sleeping. Then Pa told me she had died sometime during the night. She had complications related to Jane's birth. That's what Pa said when I asked him what happened. She looked just like she did when she was resting. But she was dead. I felt her, and she was cold. It was awful, Grandma. I started to cry, but Pa said I shouldn't cry because it's a fact of life that farm animals die, often when we least expect it. He said we have to accept death and move on. Then he said something that I'll always remember. He said that especially on a farm, we run into birth and death regularly.

Farm life may be like that, but it doesn't make me feel any better. I loved Polly. She helped me learn how to milk her when I didn't know how. She let me sit under her and tug and pull until I figured out how to make the milk come. Polly and I had our problems, too. But she became my friend. Whenever I went out to the barn, she looked at me and mooed—her way of saying, "Hello, how are you?"

Even though I knew I shouldn't cry, I had my handkerchief out of my pocket and I was wiping my eyes. I noticed that Pa was blowing his nose, too. He wouldn't let on that he felt bad about Polly, but I know he did. He liked this cow. She was gentle and gave lots of milk. I wonder if a calf feels bad when its mother dies. I fed little Jane this morning, and she didn't seem to act any differently than on other mornings. But can we always tell how animals feel? I thought about that a lot today. Even Depot didn't seem to be his bouncy self today. He saw Polly dead in her stall just like Pa and I did. I think Polly's death is affecting him, too.

A big truck came later in the day and hauled

away Polly, and now there is an empty stall in the barn. I asked Pa where the truck was taking her. He said she was going to a rendering plant. When I asked what that is, he said I should look it up in the dictionary.

It's been a sad day, Grandma.

Love,
George

Dear George,

You can't know how sorry I am to hear that your favorite cow has died. Death is never easy to understand, but it is a part of life, George. Every living thing—cow, chicken, tree—must die, some sooner, some later.

You never knew your Grandfather Struckmeyer, who died in 1919. He was only fifty years old, far too young to die. He went off to his job at the bank here in Cleveland, and he never came home. The doctor said he had a heart attack.

This happened nearly twenty years ago, and I still have trouble writing about his death. You probably are noticing the smudges on the paper—they are caused by tears. I still think about your grandfather every day, and I probably always will.

One way to make things a bit easier when a person or an animal you love dies is to think of all the good times you had together. It's hard to go on, but thinking good thoughts helps.

Your letters help me to keep going. Thank you so much for writing them.

I'm so sorry, George. Death is never easy.

Much love,
Grandma S.

May 6, 1938
Friday

Dear Grandma,

I had a hard time studying this week, but I must, because the seventh grade county tests are coming up in a few weeks. Still, all I can think about is Polly. Pa says he wants to buy another cow, but we just don't have enough money. It seems we are always short of money. I asked Pa about that, and he reminded me that the whole country is in a Depression. Lots of people have no work at all, and they have to stand in bread lines to get food, just like you described, Grandma. Pa said that we were fortunate living on a farm because we always have something to eat and plenty of milk to drink. I helped Ma plant our vegetable garden the other day, so we'll have lots of fresh vegetables by midsummer—green beans, peas, carrots, potatoes, lettuce, and tomatoes.

I'll quit asking Pa when he's going to buy another cow. Even if he does, it won't keep me from thinking about Polly. I never thought I'd miss a cow so much.

Miss Harvey seems to understand. She hasn't bawled me out for looking out the window when I should be practicing long division or studying geography.

Jane keeps growing. When I go out to the barn, the little calf runs up to the side of the pen, sticks out her tongue, and licks me. It's a strange way of saying hello, but I sure look forward to it. Jane takes my mind off Polly and reminds me of her, too, isn't that strange? She is starting to look just like her mother, especially around the eyes and muzzle. Sometimes she butts me with her head when I climb into the pen to feed her, a calf's way of having fun, I suspect. When I try to scold her, I just can't. Jane tips her head to one side and looks at me with those big dark eyes, and all I can do is laugh.

Jane seems to like Depot, too. Sometimes they stand looking at each other. Depot cocks his head to one side, and so does Jane. Is this one way animals talk to each other?

Your grandson,
George

May 7, 1938
Saturday

Dear Grandma,

A couple of weeks ago I noticed a big poster on the side of a barn as we were driving into Link Lake. The poster pictured a huge lion and a giraffe and in big red letters announced that the Ringling Brothers and Barnum & Bailey Circus is coming to Willow River, which is not that far from our farm. I've never seen a circus, and I asked Pa if we can go. He reminded me that we have lots of work to do, but he said he'll think about it.

Pa didn't say another word about going to the circus until this morning at breakfast, when he said right out of the blue that we should drive over to Willow River and see what that circus was all about. Annie burst out with a big "yippee!" I was so surprised that Pa decided that we could go, I couldn't say anything. I think even Ma was looking forward to seeing the circus, although she didn't say so. She's not one to say much, especially about things like a circus that require some extra money. She keeps track of all the money that we take in on the farm, and she questions every time Pa buys something. Circus tickets cost fifty cents for adults and twenty-five cents for kids, so it would cost our family a dollar and a half to attend.

We hurried up with our chores because Pa said we should try to get to Willow River in time to see the circus parade, which started at eleven. While I helped with the chores, I made sure not to ask why we weren't working in the fields today—Pa said just yesterday that it will soon be time to plant corn.

Willow River was running over with people who had come to see the parade and the circus performance. We found a parking place not far from Main Street and elbowed our way through the crowd to a spot where we could see the parade.

I did overhear Ma saying that maybe we should just see the parade, which was free. Pa said that as long as we were in Willow River, we might as well see the circus performance as well. Ma gave him kind of a frosty look, but there we were, about to watch the circus parade and then see the circus performance at two o'clock as well.

We hadn't waited more than ten minutes when I heard band music and saw a man on horseback riding right down the middle of Main Street. Behind the rider came an enormous wagon pulled by six horses, with a band riding on top playing wonderful music. Next was a wagon with a lion inside. He looked like he was sleeping. And then came the most exciting thing of all: elephants! At least a dozen of them marched down the street, their handlers walking alongside. I've never seen an elephant before, except in books, and are they ever big! Grandma, they are enormous! Then came the clowns, all dressed up and with their faces painted silly, some of them wearing shoes way too big for them. Annie couldn't contain herself. She was clapping and jumping up and down. I don't think I've ever seen her so happy. Even Ma was laughing.

The parade went on for nearly an hour, and when it was over, we got back in the car and drove to a big field just outside of town. The field looked like a city of tents. Pa bought our tickets at a little booth, and then we walked over toward a huge tent—Pa said it is called the Big Top. On our way there we walked through a smaller tent called the Menagerie, which is a kind of zoo, I guess. Animals from all over the world were lined up in cages: hyenas and tigers, lions and wild hogs, zebras and long-necked giraffes, and snakes that if given a chance would crush you to death and eat you for lunch. At one end of that tent, the elephants were chained to metal stakes driven in the ground. They stood there eating hay and ignoring the crowds of people walking by.

I saw Pa looking at his pocket watch, and then he motioned for us to follow him into the Big Top. Inside the tent I heard the circus band playing lively music—very different music than what I listen to on the radio coming from the WLS *Barn Dance Show* in Chicago. We found seats on bleachers that surrounded three marked-off circles in the tent, which Pa told me are called rings. The rings were maybe twenty feet across.

We'd hardly gotten settled in when I heard a loud whistle, and a man with a red coat and white pants and a tall hat walked out in the center of the one of the rings. He grabbed a microphone and in a loud voice said, "Ladies and gentlemen, children of all ages, welcome to the Ringling Brothers and Barnum & Bailey Circus!" Then, even louder, he shouted, "The greatest show on earth!"

Before the words were out of his mouth, the band was playing again and a woman rode into the ring on an elephant, followed by performers, horses, clowns—I guess everyone in the circus paraded around in front of us. All of a sudden four fancy riding horses began tearing around one of the other rings as a man with a long whip stood in the middle. With the snap of his whip, all the horses stopped, whirled around, and ran in the other direction.

Pa pointed to the center ring, and I quickly looked in that direction to see, way up in the Big Top tent, a lady on a trapeze bar swinging back and forth, back and forth. A good distance away from her, a man was swinging by his feet from another trapeze bar. Grandma, when that woman let go I was sure she would fall and be killed. But before you could snap your fingers, the man swinging across from her caught her by the wrists. It was surely something to see.

The show went on for nearly two hours, and it was just about the best thing I have ever seen. Annie was clapping and yelling nearly the whole time. Ma and Pa were grinning, and I even saw Ma laugh when a bunch of clowns crawled out of a little car. It was the first time I've seen Ma laugh since we moved to Wisconsin.

Everybody in the Big Top was having a great time. I would guess for most of them it was a rare chance to take their minds off their troubles and the Great Depression that has its grip on the country.

I didn't tell Ma or Pa this, but I think I might try some of the tricks that I saw in the Big Top yesterday. Our big cattle barn would be a good place to try them out. Our barn is a little like the Big Top, with ropes and pulleys running this way and that. I might even try to put on a circus for the neighbor kids. What do you think?

It was a good day, Grandma.

Your grandson,
George

Dear George,

How lucky you are to have seen a real circus, and the Ringling Brothers and Barnum & Bailey Circus, at that! When I was your age, the Ringling Brothers performed in our area, but I never got to see them. Your great-grandfather said we just didn't have money to waste on a circus. My brothers and I were so disappointed. But my father usually knew best.

So thank you for telling me what you saw, and what you thought of it all. I felt as if I were right there with you. It sounds like little Annie and your folks enjoyed the show, too. Sometimes we all need to put our troubles aside and see something like a circus. I'm so pleased you had a chance to have a fun day. And now you are planning to hold your own circus for the neighbor children. That sounds like so much fun. I wish I could be there to help you. Be sure to tell me what you decide to do.

Keep writing. I so enjoy hearing about all your adventures.

Love,
Grandma S.

P.S. How are things going with Amos Woodward? Is he still causing you problems?

May 8, 1938
Sunday

Dear Grandma,

Today was Mother's Day. I wanted to do something special for Ma, but I nearly got into trouble for my efforts.

When we got home from church, I asked Annie if she wanted to go with me to find a Mother's Day present. I told her not to tell Ma, and she didn't.

After the noon meal, when Ma was busy in the kitchen, I took Annie by the hand and we headed for the big woods back of the house. Pa said that he'd seen some violets at the edge of the woods, in a clearing on top of a hill. I thought Ma would be pleased if Annie and I gave her a bouquet of violets. Of course, we don't have money to buy her anything.

We went into the woods on an old logging trail that Pa told me about a while back. All the trees are shaking off the grays and browns of winter and turning many shades of green. Grandma, Annie is just filled with questions. Before we had gotten only a little ways in the woods she grabbed my hand and asked me if there are wolves there. I told her that maybe at one time there were, but not anymore. Then she asked about bears. She is really a 'fraidy cat. I told her that sometimes there might be bears around, but that we wouldn't see any. She said she surely didn't want to see a bear. I read someplace that bears are more afraid of us than we of them, and I told Annie that, but from the look on her face I knew she didn't believe me. Then I told her that the chances of us seeing a bear were about as good as having a bobcat run across the trail in front of us. I wished I hadn't mentioned bobcats, because now Annie wanted to know if one of those was around the next corner.

I pointed to a squirrel that scampered up a tree just ahead of us, and I said she should listen to the cawing of a crow that I spotted at the top of a big oak tree. But she had her little blond head fixed on wolves, bears, and bobcats. She squeezed my hand tightly as we walked, and she was humming a little tune that I couldn't identify. I asked her what it was. Here's how the discussion went:

"A song," she said.

I told her I knew it was a song and asked what song.

"I'm not telling," she said.

"Why not?"

"'Cause you'll laugh."

"I won't laugh," I told her.

"A keep-the-bears-away song," she whispered.

"You and your bears," I said.

"You said you wouldn't laugh."

I told her I wasn't laughing, only smiling. We had been climbing for a while, and now we came to the top of a hill to an opening where no trees or underbrush grow. I told Annie to look at the ground.

"Posies," she said.

"They're violets, Annie. Aren't they pretty?"

I showed her how to pick them so the stems would be long enough for Ma to put them in a water glass. Soon we each had a fine bouquet of violets, mostly dark purple, but some with lavender petals. I told Annie to hold them tight, but not too tight.

We headed toward home, thoughts of bears, wolves, and bobcats forgotten.

I was sure Ma would be surprised. She had spotted us coming out of the woods, and she was waiting for us on the porch. Right away she asked where we had been. She said she had been worried sick about us, and she looked really mad. Then she looked right at me and said, "George, you know you're not supposed to go into the woods. You should know better. What if something happened to you and Annie?"

I didn't know what to say, so I just walked up to her and handed her the bouquet of violets and said, "Happy Mother's Day."

Annie did the same, only she said, "Happy 'other's Day."

I have never seen such a surprised look on Ma's face. One minute she looked very angry, then she looked surprised, and then she burst into tears. She hugged each of us and said, "Thank you, thank you. What a perfect Mother's Day." She put both of our bouquets in glasses of water and set them in the middle of the kitchen table.

That was a close one, Grandma. But it turned out to be a good day.

Your grandson,
George

May 9, 1938
Monday

Dear Grandma,

Pa sure is full of surprises. After school today, while I was doing my evening barn chores, the big red truck that had delivered our cows and horses drove into our yard. I've gotten to know the driver a little; Ross

Caves is his name. Mr. Caves stepped down from the truck and asked if Pa was around. I said he was in the barn and I'd go fetch him. When I told Pa the trucker was here and wanted to see him, he started smiling—just a little smile that Pa sometimes gets when he is feeling good about something.

"Hello there, Adolph," the trucker said. "Where do you want me to unload him?"

Now I wondered what Pa had bought. We already have horses and cows, and Ma has her chickens. I thought maybe Pa had bought a hog somewhere. Mr. Caves let down the ramp at the back of the truck and walked inside. When he appeared again at the top of the ramp, he was leading a pony, a little Shetland. Slowly Mr. Caves and the pony walked down the ramp, and then he handed the halter rope to me and said that this must be my new pony. It sure wasn't a hog.

I took the rope, but I just stood there looking dumb. I don't know anything about ponies. Pa asked about the pony's name.

"Ginger," said Mr. Caves. "He's been injured at one time or another—you can see his front knees are overly large—and he's pretty old. But otherwise he seems okay. Very gentle. Seems to like people."

Ginger stood beside me, not moving, just looking at me as if to say, "Who are you?" I rubbed his forehead with my free hand, which he seemed to like, as he moved his head up and down against my hand.

Mr. Caves put up the ramp, crawled into his truck, waved goodbye, and drove away. When the truck was out of sight, I asked if this was really my pony. Pa said it is but I will have to share Ginger with

Annie, and because I am older it will be my responsibility to take care of him.

I asked Pa where he had found the pony. Pa explained that Ginger was a circus pony and had performed for several years with the Ringling Brothers and Barnum & Bailey Circus. But he is getting old, so the circus sold him to Mr. Caves. Mr. Caves knew Pa has kids and thought he might be interested. Pa said he paid only ten dollars for Ginger.

Now Annie came running from the house, yelling at the top of her lungs, "It's a pony! It's a pony! Can I ride him? Can I ride him?"

Pa lifted Annie onto Ginger's back and told her to hold onto his mane so she wouldn't fall off. Then I led Ginger around the yard a couple times, with Annie holding on tight and grinning from ear to ear.

Pa said Mr. Caves told him Ginger knows a bunch of tricks. I asked what kind of tricks—I'm still thinking about putting on my own circus, and having a pony do tricks will surely make it more interesting. Pa said we'll wait a few days for Ginger to get acquainted with his new surroundings, and then we'll see what tricks he knows.

After a few turns around the yard, Pa said that Ginger was probably tired after arriving on the circus train to Willow River and then being trucked out here to the farm. Annie slid off him and I led him into the barn and tied him in his new stall, which Pa built in the barn while I was at school today.

Imagine, Grandma, now I have both a dog and a pony. What more could a kid want?

Your grandson,
George

Dear George,

Have you ever heard of a "dog and pony show?" Well, now that's just what you can do with the circus you are planning. And you have a real circus pony—how lucky can you be? I'll bet your little sister is just smiling like everything. I know I would be if I had both a puppy and a pony.

Do you know yet what kinds of tricks your pony can do? When you find out, let me know.

Congratulations. You are a lucky boy!

Love,
Grandma S.

May 11, 1938
Wednesday

Dear Grandma,

Our school plays Forest Grove School in softball next week. Forest Grove won last year 7 to 6, and Miss Harvey says we can't let that happen again. Our team practices every noon and every recess, too. I don't practice much, though. I can't run fast enough to play any of the positions well. At least I don't fall down as often anymore. I guess my leg is getting a little better. But Amos still thinks I shouldn't be on the team.

Rachel asked me last week if I'd like to be the team pitcher. She told me that pitchers don't have to move around much, and she said that she knew I could do it. I told her I'd like to try, so every night after chores I've been practicing out back of the pump house. Miss Harvey said I can take the softball home overnight, if I remember to bring it back every morning.

I drew a circle on the side of the pump house with some chalk, backed up the correct distance, and practiced hitting the target. At first I didn't even come close, but after a while I was hitting the circle right in the middle about two out of three tries. Now I've got to work on pitching faster. When I pitched at recess today almost everyone hit the ball, even the second-graders. I've got to do better so I can strike them out. They shouldn't be able to hit so easily.

Your grandson,
George

May 20, 1938
Friday

Dear Grandma,

What a ball game it was! We played at Forest Grove School. Their ball diamond is in a little field out back of their school, and it crowds up to a big oak woods. It's mostly flat ground, which makes it better than our diamond, where we have to run uphill to get to second base (of course then it's downhill to home plate—if we get that far).

Grandma, these kids can play ball as well as they can spell. They can hit, and they run like deer. There were a lot of mothers at the game, cheering for both sides. I was so happy to see my mother and little Annie. Grandma Woodward came, too. I asked one of the kids where Amos's mother was, and he told me that she died when Amos was a baby. Grandma Woodward is quite a lady. You should have seen her standing along the first base line, waving her arms and cheering every time our team got a hit or somebody caught a fly ball. Sure helps to have somebody cheering. Little Annie got into that, too. She cheered no matter who hit the ball, their team or our team.

I was the starting pitcher. Grandma, I struck out the first kid that came up to the plate! I figured he must be one of their best players, or they wouldn't have had him bat first. I think he was a little anxious and swung early. I still haven't learned how to throw very fast, but Miss Harvey showed me how to hold the ball so that it drops or climbs when I pitch it, depending on how I throw it. It took maybe three innings before these Forest Grove kids caught on to what I heard one of them say is a strange way of pitching.

Herman—that same tall, skinny kid with the badly worn overalls who can spell so well—was the first one to hit one of my sinkers. He whaled on it! Herman sent the ball flying past second base and got himself a double.

As usual, whenever I came up to bat I either hit the ball high in the air and somebody caught it, or I hit it on the ground. By the time I limped to first base, their first baseman was standing there with the ball, waiting for me. It was embarrassing, but it didn't bother me quite as much as it once did.

I kept on pitching until the seventh inning. By then I was getting mighty tired. Amos wanted to pull me after the Forest Grove kid hit a double on my sinker ball, but Rachel said no, that I should stay in a little longer. I don't know how Rachel does it, but she talks back to Amos, and he listens.

At the eighth inning, the score was tied 5 to 5. Forest Grove got another run in the ninth. Now we had just three more chances to tie the game and maybe even win. I was beginning to think that the ball game was going to turn out just like the spelling bee.

Grandma Woodward, Ma, and Annie kept cheering us on. Grandma Woodward waved a little red handkerchief as she yelled. I was surprised that the Forest Grove teacher didn't tell her to quit shaking that handkerchief and sit down, but she didn't.

Amos was up to bat. For all his faults—and he's got lots of them—he's a good ball player. He can really hit. His grandma was yelling, "Hit it into the woods! Hit it into the woods!" Amos looked over at her and said, "I'll try, Grandma." I've noticed that Amos has a different way of talking to his grandmother. He's always polite, and he doesn't say anything nasty like he does when he talks to me and some of the other kids.

Amos stood up to the plate and glared down at the new Forest Grove pitcher, a girl who came up only to his shoulder. One thing I noticed about this pitcher, besides seeing that she is just about the cutest girl in their school, was her fastball. Her name is Amy, and she can pitch a softball twice as fast as I can. Herman is their catcher—his hands are as big as sofa pillows—and even he shakes his hands after this cute pitcher whistles in one of her fast pitches. The ball must sting something fierce. (Nobody on either team wears gloves of any kind, not even the catcher. And the teachers trade off calling balls and strikes. It sure is different from how we played ball in Ohio.)

Amy's first pitch sailed right by Amos. He took a mighty cut at it—and nearly fell down in the process.

"Strike one," the Forest Grove teacher yelled.

Amos was embarrassed. He picked up a handful of dirt, rubbed his hands together, grabbed the bat, and stepped back up to the plate. He waved the bat across the plate a couple times and yelled to the pitcher, "Show me what you got." The pitcher did, and Amos got another strike.

His face got redder and redder. It is one thing to miss the ball, but to miss a ball pitched by a girl must have been too much for Amos to endure.

Meanwhile, Grandma Woodward was still cheering for him, yelling, "You can do it, Amos!"

Amos didn't respond. This time he spit on one hand and then the other before grabbing the bat and stepping to the plate. He pointed his bat out toward the woods, I suspect to intimidate the pitcher. So far nothing had upset her.

The next pitch was a fastball right down the middle. The Forest Grove pitcher didn't know it, but the fastball is Amos's favorite pitch. He pulled back the bat and swung. "Crack!" That ball went sailing higher and higher, toward the big woods behind the outfield. One of Forest Grove School's outfielders ran as fast as he could toward where he figured the ball would fall. He had only a few feet left to go and he'd be in the woods, and nobody can catch a ball in the woods. Then the outfielder stopped, held up his hands, and caught the ball. "You're out!" yelled the Forest Grove teacher.

Grandma, you should have seen the look on Amos's face. He figured he had hit a home run for sure. He threw down his bat and stomped off the field. I could hear him cussing, and I hoped Miss Harvey heard him, too. If you get caught swearing at our school, Miss Harvey lays down the law, which usually means sweeping out the boy's outhouse for a couple months.

Rachel was up next. She hit a little dribbler that rolled far enough so she had time to get on first.

"Tying run on first," yelled Grandma Woodward. I noticed she had walked over to where Amos was sitting with his head in his hands and was talking to him.

Amy struck out our next player. We had one chance left. Rachel yelled from first base for me to bat. Amos was beside himself. He said something, but I didn't hear it because I was busy stepping up to the plate to face the cute pitcher from Forest Grove School who never smiled, never frowned, never said a word, just pitched. One fast pitch after the other.

By this time everyone on both teams knew about my bad leg, and most everyone must have been wondering why Rachel picked me to bat. I knew that unless I hit a home run, I would be thrown out at first.

I limped up to home plate and waved the bat a couple times. I had no more than gathered my thoughts when I heard the ball slam into the catcher's hands.

"Strike one," the Forest Grove teacher yelled.

The next time I was ready when I stepped up to the plate. Another fastball. I hit it a little on the side, and it climbed high enough, but it dropped foul. Strike two.

"You can do it, Georgie," yelled Annie. Grandma, you know I don't let anybody call me Georgie except Annie and my mother, and then only on rare occasions.

I thought maybe Amos had the right idea when he picked up some dirt and rubbed it between his fingers before grabbing the bat, so I did the same, but the only thing that happened was I got dust in my nose and I sneezed.

"God bless you," said the Forest Grove teacher.

I rubbed my dirty hand across my nose, picked up the bat, and limped up to the plate. I could see drops of sweat on the pitcher's forehead. She wound up and let go with another one of her fastballs, probably the fastest ball she had pitched all day. If she struck me out they would win the game just like they did last year. Our school would never hear the last of it. We couldn't let Forest Grove School win the spelling bee *and* the ball game.

I closed my eyes and swung with everything I had, and the bat hit the ball. I opened my eyes to see the ball going higher and higher and heading for the woods. The question was, had I hit it hard enough for a home run, or would one of their outfield speedsters catch it? Two outfielders were racing toward where they figured it would fall.

Grandma, that ball fell a good twenty feet into the woods.

"Home run!" yelled our team and everyone on the side rooting for us. "Home run! Our team wins. Our team wins!"

I can't remember when I've felt more proud. I limped around the bases as fast as I could, making sure I stepped on each one. Our entire team stood waiting for me at home plate so they could pat me on the back or shake my hand—all except Amos Woodward. He just stood there sneering. Amos almost spoiled what was a near perfect day.

Your grandson,
George

Dear George,

Thank you so much for your long and detailed letter about the ball game. I felt I was right there with you at the game.

I'm sorry Amos Woodward is still a problem for you. From what you said about the spelling bee, it sounds like his Pa is really hard on him. I'm sure that's part of the reason he thinks he has to pick on somebody else. I think he is angry about his life. Do you think that is so?

I'm impressed that even with your bum leg you were able to hit a home run. My father always said to me, "Do the best you can with what you've got," and you are surely doing that. Just because you can't run doesn't mean you can't do other things. You've proved that.

I'm glad you're feeling proud of yourself. It's important to do that once in a while, especially when other things aren't going so well.

Love,
Grandma S.

May 21, 1938
Saturday

Dear Grandma,

Ginger knows all kinds of tricks. He stands on his hind legs, waving his front legs in the air. He can even stand on a box on just his front legs. And he's so gentle that Annie rides him all over the place. I'm trying to teach Depot some tricks as well, but all that interests him is playing. I must say, both Annie and I have lots of fun playing with that little dog. One of his favorite games is having Annie chase him. He runs around in a big circle, barking his puppy bark. Then Annie runs after him, and then he runs after Annie. Grandma, you are right: it sure is fun to have both a pony and a puppy.

The other day when I was working with Ginger, Pa reminded me that the pony is a lot older than the puppy. "You've got to take it a little easy with Ginger," Pa said. "Remember, he's not a spring chicken anymore." (By that Pa meant Ginger is old.)

I mentioned to Pa my idea of having a circus, and he didn't say no. So now I'm trying to figure out just what my circus will be about. With my bad leg, I can't do any running, but I've been practicing swinging on a rope from one big beam in the barn to another, sort of like the circus acrobats did. My arms are strong, and with a little more practice I should have this trick ready. Ginger has some good tricks to show off, too. And I think I can put together a reasonable menagerie with some of the animals around the farm, both tame and wild.

I'm really looking forward to doing the circus. It should be lots of fun. I'd sure like you to see it.

Your grandson,
George

May 23, 1938
Monday

Dear Grandma,

After school today I helped Grandma Woodward with her garden. She called Ma on the party line telephone and wondered if I could bring over the team of horses, level off her garden with the smoothing drag, and help her plant. Pa said it would be all right, if I was careful. He helped me load one section of the spike-toothed smoothing drag on the stone boat. I stood on the stone boat, holding tight to the leather lines that control the horses. With Maud and Tony walking in front of me, carrying their heads high and swishing their long tails to drive away the flies that make life miserable for animals this time of year, I felt like a Roman gladiator must have felt driving a chariot with a team prancing in front. I was feeling good about being asked to do some work for a neighbor with the horses, even if it was only leveling off a little garden spot with the smoothing drag.

Grandma Woodward seemed glad to see me come into the yard with the team.

I asked her to hold the lines while I unloaded the drag from the stone boat. Soon I had the team hitched to the drag, and within just a few minutes, Grandma Woodward's garden spot was as smooth as a beach at the lake.

I tied the team to a fence post and asked, "What next?" Grandma Woodward said next we must mark the rows. She has a homemade wooden marker that I figure has been around nearly as long as Grandma Woodward. It makes two little furrows in the soil when you pull it across the garden, which I did, back and forth, until her entire plot was a series of little furrows stretching from one end to the other.

While I was working, she told me how much she appreciated my help. Then she said, "My grandson, Amos, is a good boy, too. But his pa keeps him so busy working that he doesn't have time to come over and help me."

Whenever she brings up Amos, I don't know what to say. Sometimes I wonder if we are talking about the same kid. From my perspective, he is mostly mean and doesn't care about other people at all.

Then we talked about the ball game against Forest Grove School. She said I was some kind of hero for hitting the winning home run. I said I just got lucky, because they have a really good pitcher. She said it was more than luck and that it is too bad I have a gimpy leg, as I could be a really good ball player. I thanked her and said that I appreciated that she had come and cheered for us.

Now that the garden plot was ready, Grandma Woodward picked up her box of garden seeds from next to her rocking chair and said we should start with the peas.

She showed me how to use a hoe to make the furrow a little deeper and then place the pea seeds in the furrow, one after the other and only a couple inches apart. Then she showed me how to cover the seeds and firm the soil with my shoe. "Got to have a firm seedbed," she said.

Next I planted radish seeds with carrot seeds mixed in. "I'll pull the radishes when they are ready, and then the carrots will grow in their place. That way I can get two crops in one row," Grandma Woodward told me.

Next came beets, green beans, sweet corn, cucumbers, squash, and pumpkins. She saved three rows, two for potatoes and one for tomatoes. She said she already has tomato plants growing in the house and will wait a couple weeks before setting them out. "Might still have a frosty night, and that would kill the tomatoes for sure," she said.

Next we turned to planting potatoes. Pa has

shown me how to cut the seed potatoes into smaller pieces, making sure there is an eye (a growing point) on every cut piece. I cut all of Grandma Woodward's seed potatoes, dug holes with the hoe along the assigned garden rows, and put a piece of seed potato in each hole. Then I filled each one with soil and stamped it with my foot.

All the while I was working, Grandma Woodward was making little markers that she stuck in the ground at the end of each row. They will remind her what crop is growing where.

Gardens sure are a lot of work, Grandma. But it was fun to work with Grandma Woodward. She showed me just what to do and didn't get upset when I didn't do it just right. I told her that when I'm working with Pa, if I don't do something right he sometimes yells at me. "Fathers are like that sometimes," Grandma Woodward said. She laughed a little. I wondered if she was thinking about Amos's father, who seems to yell at Amos a lot.

It was quiet in Grandma Woodward's garden. I heard a meadowlark call from the hayfield across the way. I really like the sound of the spring birds.

Thanks for your last letter. I always like hearing from you. Pa and Ma like reading your letters, too. Pa would never say so, but sometimes I think he misses Ohio more than I do.

Love,
George

Dear George,

Grandma Woodward surely sounds like a nice person. I'm so pleased to hear that you've found some time to help her with her garden. Older people sometimes need a little extra help with things like putting in a garden. And do you know what? I'll bet you are learning some things from Grandma Woodward as well, maybe without even knowing you are doing so.

On my home farm, we always had a big vegetable garden. Here in Cleveland I can grow only a few things, like a short row of lettuce and a tomato plant or two that I plant next to the garage. From your good description it sounds like Grandma Woodward has lots of room for a garden. She's fortunate.

Keep the letters coming.

Love,
Grandma S.

May 27, 1938
Friday

Dear Grandma,

Today was our last day of school for the year, and what a fun day it was! Miss Harvey told us we didn't have to come to school until noon today, and she sent notes home inviting our parents to come, too, for a picnic dinner.

I don't think I told you about the end-of-term exams. Because I'm in seventh grade, I had to take county exams in geography and arithmetic. I passed both of them with high grades. I did a lot of studying in my spare time. Miss Harvey said she has never had a seventh grade student fail the county tests, and she didn't want me to be the first. I surely didn't want to be the first one, either. I could just hear people in the neighborhood, especially Amos Woodward, shouting about how this limpy city kid from Ohio flunked seventh grade. But I didn't fail, and now I'll be going into eighth grade next year.

Amos (I couldn't believe it) and Rachel passed their eighth grade exams, and both are headed for Link Lake High School next fall. I say, good riddance to Amos Woodward, although I imagine the softball team will suffer some without him. I know we'll miss Rachel. She's a good ballplayer and treats everybody fairly. That's more than you can say about Amos.

When we got to the schoolhouse today, many of the students and their parents were already there. I saw Rachel, and I went over to congratulate her on passing the county exams. She said the same to me, even though I had taken exams in only two subjects, and she had taken examinations in every subject. Besides that, the eighth-graders had to take the county exams at the County Normal School in Willow River, where teachers go for training. Rachel said she took exams all day, one after the other, and it was about the worst thing she's ever done. I told her high school will probably be easy after all that. She said she's a little scared about going to high school, because the town kids and the country kids will be all mixed together. She's heard that the town kids make fun of the country kids, calling them names like "hayseeds" and "hicks." I told her I didn't know anything about that; all I know is that city kids get teased when they go to a country school.

"Not everybody teased you," she said.

"You and some of the little first- and second-graders were about the only ones who didn't," I said. She smiled.

I went back to where Ma and Pa were standing, near a long table made out of planks and sawhorses that the school board had set up. That's where Ma put the bowl of potato salad she had made—right next to all kinds of other bowls and pans and dishes of food. Ma also brought along sandwiches for us to eat and plates, glasses, knives, and forks.

Miss Harvey welcomed everybody and told us to get in line for food. She said that since it was a special day for the eighth-graders, who are going on to high school next year, they and their parents should be the first in line.

Ma, Pa, Annie, and I got in line behind one of the first-graders and his folks and started filling our plates. What a spread of food! There were baked beans, green Jell-O with sliced bananas on top, several kinds of potato salad (some with slices of boiled eggs on top), sauerkraut and wieners, fried chicken, sliced ham, deviled eggs, dill pickles, scalloped potatoes, and hamburger casserole. And on the far end of the table, near a huge bucket of lemonade with a dipper hanging on the side, were the desserts: apple, cherry, lemon, and blackberry pie. Chocolate, yellow, marble, and cherry cake. Sugar cookies, peanut butter cookies, and molasses cookies (I've never liked them, but Pa says molasses cookies are his favorite).

By the time I got through the line, I could hardly carry my plate, it was so full. Grandma Woodward was in the line behind us, and while I was dipping some lemonade into my glass, she asked me if I forgot to eat yesterday. Then she smiled that big smile that pushes back the wrinkles in her face. I smiled back.

At our school it's a tradition that all the kids play softball against the fathers on the last day, and after we finished eating, that's what we did. What a hoot. I don't think most of the fathers had played ball since the last school picnic. But that sure didn't keep them from trying.

I was so proud of Pa. He just grabbed hold of the bat and walked right up to the plate, swinging it like he knew what he was doing. Know what, Grandma? It was the first time I've ever seen Pa play a game, any kind of game. He's either working or he's resting. I have never, ever seen him play ball before.

Since our big ball game with Forest Grove School, we've all kept right on playing every recess at noon. I've been working on my sinker and my riser (that's what Miss Harvey calls my pitch that climbs). I told Pa that I've been pitching, but I don't think it sunk in—until he stepped up to the plate, and there he was, facing me. He had the strangest look on his face.

One of the little kids yelled, "Strike him out!" I don't think the little guy knew that the batter was my Pa.

I tossed one of my sinker balls. Pa took a mighty swing and hit the ball higher than any of the kids could have. But Rachel was right there to catch it, and Pa was out. He looked a little surprised as he sat down under a shade tree with the other fathers.

Amos's pa, Mr. Woodward, was up next. He's a big burly fellow with a bald head, a black beard, and arms as big as oak trees. He has a reputation as a good ball player; before the game the other kids told me that the father's team can always depend on Mr. Woodward to hit a home run when he steps up to the plate.

"Amos told me about you, kid," he said to me as he picked up the bat.

I figured Amos had told his pa about my bad leg and that it was the reason I was the pitcher and not shagging fly balls in the outfield.

"Let's see what you got, kid," Mr. Woodward said, slowly swinging the bat across the plate. That bat looked like a piece of kindling wood in Mr. Woodward's big hands.

I wound up like I was going to throw a fastball, and then I let go with my sinker. Mr. Woodward made a powerful swing at the ball and missed it entirely. He came near to falling down.

"Say, Woodward, looks like there's a hole in your bat," one of the fathers yelled.

Mr. Woodward muttered something I couldn't hear—I suspect they were words that would send Miss Harvey into fits if one of her students had spoken them. Then Amos's pa said it was just a lucky pitch.

I decided to try one of my risers, and he missed that one, too. By this time he had a menacing look on his face. Mr. Woodward spit on both hands, grabbed the bat, and glared down at me with a glare like I have never seen. He looked like he was ready to hit the ball into the next county, or at least into the next school district.

I figured Mr. Woodward would either be expecting my sinker or my riser, so I decided to send one right down the middle with as much steam as I could put on it. I am not known for my fastball, but it has gotten better as the ball season has progressed.

I could see Mr. Woodward eyeing the ball in my hands, the muscles in his arms jerking, waiting for it to come across the plate. I wound up in my usual way and let go of the ball, except this time I threw it as hard as I could. I could see that it was going to fly right across the plate, a perfect pitch.

All the kids in school were standing off to the side, watching and hoping that I would strike out Mr. Woodward.

"Swoosh." Everyone heard the bat miss the ball, but no one expected what happened next. Mr. Woodward completely lost his balance and fell in a heap right across the board that is our home plate. A little cloud of dust lifted from around his massive body, and then it was quiet for a few seconds. Grandma, I swear I heard birds chirping, it was so quiet.

Then Mr. Woodward scrambled to his feet, brushed off the dust, and swore so loudly that I was sure Miss Harvey didn't miss a word. I imagine some of the younger kids have never heard such high-powered swearing in their lives.

Before Mr. Woodward could complete his litany of cuss words—frankly, I've never known one man to have such a swearing vocabulary—the fathers began laughing, and then they were howling. They were slapping their knees and hooting and pointing at me and at Mr. Woodward. I just stood on the little pitcher's mound with a little grin on my face.

Then Amos walked over to me from where he was playing second base and said under his breath so only I could hear, "I'm gonna get you for this, Struckmeyer. You'll wish you hadn't made a fool of my old man." He stomped back to second.

Mr. Woodward hit a home run the next time he was up to bat, and the fathers ended up winning the game—apparently they do every year. Some of the fathers told me afterward that I am the first kid ever to strike out Mr. Woodward.

Amos is really mad. I hope I don't run into him this summer.

Your grandson,
George

May 31, 1938
Tuesday

Dear Grandma,

It's a good thing school is out, because Pa has so much work around the farm that he can't keep up with it. The weather has cooperated so that the corn is up and needs cultivating (that means removing the weeds). The potato patch is full of weeds, too, and

Ma's garden needs hoeing. And Pa says that before we know it we'll be making hay. Making hay is cutting the hay plants, allowing them to dry, and then hauling them to the barn where we store the hay. We will feed the dried hay to the cattle and horses this winter.

Yesterday Pa said it was high time we cultivated the potatoes. He planted about three acres of potatoes at one end of the cornfield back in April, and now they are knee high and growing well—but the weeds are growing even faster than the potatoes.

We've got two horse-drawn cultivators. A cultivator consists of a set of small shovels that plow little furrows between the rows, plus two handles that you steer it with. As the cultivator moves along, the little shovels either dig up or bury most of the weeds. Whatever the cultivator doesn't get, we have to hoe out by hand, a tedious, backbreaking job. Pa hitched Maud to one cultivator and Tony to the other. He asked me to drive Maud—she's a little less skittish than Tony is.

As with every other job on the farm, there is a trick to cultivating with a one-horse cultivator. What you really need is four arms: two to hold the leather lines to steer the horse, and two more to hold onto the handles and guide the cultivator between the rows. Pa showed me how to tie the lines together so I can slip them over my neck and keep my hands free to hold the cultivator handles. He had me practice a little at the ends of the rows, where no potatoes grow. I quickly discovered if I pushed on the cultivator handles in the direction I wanted the cultivator to go, it went in the opposite direction. Not only did I have to make my two arms seem like four, I had to make my mind think in opposites!

Pa got me started between two rows of potatoes. Maud plodded along and didn't require any steering until I got to the end of the row. I concentrated on guiding the cultivator so it dug out the largest amount of weeds without killing any potatoes. A couple of times I got too close to the row and dug up a few potato plants; if Pa noticed, he didn't say anything. I guess he knows how hard it is to steer a cultivator pulled by a horse.

Cultivating potatoes isn't fun. But if you like being outside under a bright sun, and if you like the smell of freshly turned soil mingling with the smells of harness leather and horse sweat, then it has some good moments. I didn't think I would ever say this, but I kind of like all these smells and sights on the farm. I enjoy the sounds, too. It was mostly quiet out there in the potato patch, except for the scraping sound of the cultivator as it moved through the soil and clanged once in a while when it struck a stone that we didn't find earlier this spring. Harness leather creaks in an interesting way, and sometimes when I got to the end of a row, Maud would whinny at Tony over at the opposite end of the patch. I suspect it was horse talk: "How are you doing? I'm doing all right so far. I think George is finally catching on."

Every half hour or so we rested the horses under a shade tree at the end of a row. I needed the rest as much as the horses did. Even with two good legs, cultivating would be hard work. For me it was a real challenge. I stumbled along behind the cultivator, holding onto the handles, which gave me some support. I have noticed, though, that my leg doesn't hurt as much as it used to. But I'm still limping.

About midmorning the sun turned on the heat. Sweat dripped off my chin and soaked my shirt, as it did Maud's hide, but we kept on cultivating, digging up and burying weeds so the potatoes will have a better chance to amount to something. Then I noticed that the cultivator had turned up a strange-looking stone. It was greenish and about the size of a man's fist, but with a little part sticking out like a handle. I kicked it with my foot, and it scarcely moved.

"Whoa," I said to Maud, and I bent over to pick up the stone. It was heavy, about twice the weight I was expecting it to be, based on its size. I carried the green stone to the end of the row and tossed it under a tree. The next time we stopped the horses for a rest, I showed it to Pa. He said he had never seen a stone like it. He even wondered if it might be gold! I wasn't sure if he was kidding or not.

"We'd be rich," I said.

"Yes, we would," he said, and he ran his hands over the surface of the object. He took out his jackknife and scraped off some of the green. Underneath, the material sparkled in the sun. I asked him if he still thought it was gold.

"Might be," Pa said. "Professor Amundson would know. He knows about these things."

I've heard about Professor Oliver Amundson from some of the neighbors. They all talk about how strange he is. He's retired from a college in southern Wisconsin and lives in a little house east of Link Lake where he grows a big garden and reads lots of books.

Last night after we finished the chores, Pa and I drove over to Professor Amundson's house. He is a big burly man but is kind of hunched over when he walks. He has a full white beard, and his head is covered with long white hair that he ties together at the back of his neck with a black string. (I must say, nobody else around here wears their hair like that, especially not the men.)

We introduced ourselves, and then Pa handed him the green stone. He asked him straight out if we found a hunk of gold. Grandma, the whole time I had my fingers crossed, hoping it was gold, but after touching the stone and holding it up close to his eyes, the professor said, "Copper."

Pa asked him if he was sure it was copper, and the professor said he was certain. He said that the hunk of copper we have is nearly pure, and he asked where we found it. Pa told him and asked if we might have more copper on our farm.

"Not likely," the professor answered. He explained that a long time ago, Indians probably lost the piece of copper while they were passing through the land that is now our farm. They used copper to make arrowheads. Professor Amundson said they likely got it from the Upper Peninsula of Michigan, where there's lots of copper.

I asked him if the piece of copper I found is valuable. He said it's worth a few dollars, but it's probably worth more in "historical significance." I didn't quite know what he meant by that, but it surely has something to do with the Indians who roamed over our farm many, many years ago. So guess what, Grandma? I now have a piece of copper on the dresser next to my bed. Cultivating potatoes turned out to be more interesting than just walking behind Maud and digging up weeds.

Thanks for your last letter and for the picture you enclosed. Ma put it in a little frame, and it now stands right next to my piece of Indian copper. I look at your picture when I write my letters to you.

Your grandson,
George

June 5, 1938
Sunday

Dear Grandma,

When I have some spare time—which happens only in the evenings when the chores are done and on Sunday afternoons—I've been practicing for my circus. I've decided to call it the Struckmeyer Stupendous Family Circus. I've been making posters with crayons. They don't look near as fancy as the Ringling Brothers posters I saw in Link Lake, but they are fun to make. I cut a picture of a lion out of an old magazine and pasted it on one poster, and I pasted a picture of a snake on another. I asked Pa what would be a good day to put on the circus, and he suggested the afternoon of Sunday, June 26. He said the barn will still be mostly empty then, because haying season would just be starting.

June 26 is only three weeks away, so I've been very busy. Annie is helping, too, but there is only so much a three-year-old can do. I asked Rachel

Williams if she would like to have her pet raccoon, Gregory, perform in our circus, and she said yes, so now we have one more act in our show. I'll bet it'll be a good one, too, for Gregory knows a whole bunch of tricks. Ginger and Depot seem excited, too. Can animals look forward to something, Grandma?

I haven't told you much about Link Lake, where we buy groceries and where Ma takes her eggs. Now that summer is here, we go to Link Lake every Saturday night, after we finish chores and take baths. Saturday night is bath night all year long. Now that the weather is warm, Pa puts our galvanized metal bathtub in the woodshed. That way our baths aren't as messy as when we take them in the kitchen in front of the stove.

Pa and I must carry the water from the pump house into the kitchen to be heated on the stove, in the little water storage area at one side of the cooking area. Now we must carry the heated water back outside and into the woodshed as well.

We take our baths in order of our age, first little Annie, then me, then Ma, and finally Pa. Ma makes us bathe with a powerful smelling soap called Lifebuoy. You can tell who has taken a bath with Lifebuoy for hours afterward. It's not a bad smell—nothing like chicken manure, for instance. It's more of a clean smell that lets you know you've had a bath and scrubbed away the dirt from a week of farm work.

Last night, after we were all scrubbed and in our clean clothes, we piled into our old car. There was just enough room for Ma and Pa in the front, and Annie, me, and a crate of eggs in the back. Ma trades her eggs for groceries at the Link Lake Mercantile, which is on Main Street. Besides having groceries, the mercantile sells clothing, shoes, thread, needles, barn boots, winter caps, leather gloves, fabric of various colors, and even toy wagons, sleds, and checkerboards.

Down the street from the mercantile is Johnson's Hardware. Pa and I usually go to Johnson's while Ma takes Annie to the mercantile. All the farmers gather at Johnson's, sitting either around a big stove in the back room in winter or on the worn wooden bench out front in summer.

Next to Johnson's is Stevens's Drugstore, where you can buy a double-dip ice cream cone for five cents and two sticks of gum for a penny. Pa gives me a nickel every Saturday night. I can spend it any way I want—which usually means a big strawberry ice cream cone. I can't think of anything that tastes better than strawberry ice cream. Steven's also has packaged ice cream to take home, but we don't have electricity and a refrigerator, so we have no place to keep it.

Link Lake has a clothing store, a blacksmith's shop (Pa brings his broken machinery there for repair), a restaurant where the sign says you can buy a plate lunch for fifty cents with coffee thrown in, a harness shop, and three taverns. Pa doesn't like taverns. I haven't figured out what he's got against them. He's not against beer drinking—in fact, he usually has a couple bottles of beer in our icebox. (Our icebox is like a refrigerator, except you can't plug it in because there's no electricity. A block of ice sits in the top of the icebox to keep the food and drink cold.)

Link Lake also has a bank, a post office, a barber shop, and a gas station next to a used car dealer that doesn't seem to be doing any business these days. The grist mill that grinds our cow feed is on the edge of town, next to the dam by the millpond.

Summer Saturday nights in Link Lake are special besides the strawberry ice cream and gum, two sticks for a penny; free movies are shown as soon as it gets dark. Across Main Street from Steven's Drugstore is an open area that slants toward the millpond. Wooden planks nailed to blocks of wood are lined up for seats, and the movie screen is a big white sheet hung on a wooden frame on the shore of the millpond.

By the time it's dark, you can't find a soul on the sidewalks, the stores empty out, and even the tavern dwellers make their way to the open-air theater to watch whatever is showing—usually a western movie. Before the main feature, the projectionist shows a serial film. That's the kind with a story that continues on from week to week. Just when the hero is up against the worst kind of disaster (last night he was about to go over a waterfall), the film quits and a little sign says "Continued Next Week." It's one way to keep us coming to town every Saturday night, I guess. I surely want to know what happened to the guy in the white hat who was tumbling over the waterfall to certain death.

Unfortunately, the evening wasn't as much fun as I have made it sound so far. In the middle of the main feature, I had to visit the outhouse. I made my way down toward the millpond, where the outhouse is located behind a tavern. As bad luck would have it, I met up with Amos Woodward, who must have been doing the same thing I was. He was the last person I wanted to meet. The first thing he said when he saw me was, "I ought to knock your head off." He walked right up to me, blocking my way to the outhouse.

I told him I didn't want to fight. He said I deserve a thrashing because I made a fool out of his pa at the school picnic. I told him that all I did was strike out his pa. Amos bristled up and said that nobody strikes out his old man, especially not some limpy little city kid.

I told him to leave me alone and that I didn't want any trouble. He said that I should roll up my sleeves and fight like a man. I said once more that I didn't want to fight. Then I saw that he had made his hands into fists and was bringing back his arm to hit me. Just as he swung, I ducked and moved to the side. Amos shot right past me and fell in the millpond with a huge splash. The people in the first row watching the movie saw what happened. I just walked away, but I could hear Amos spitting and sputtering and saying something about how he is gonna get me. I hurried on to the outhouse. When I got back, Amos was nowhere in sight. Looks like I've really got to watch out for him now. I'm worried about Amos. Any ideas about what I should do?

Keep writing. I like getting your letters.

Your grandson,
George

Dear George,

Link Lake sounds like such an interesting town. From your description, it has just about everything your family needs. And watching a free outdoor movie in summer—what a fun thing that must be!

That brings me once more to your problems with Amos. I know you probably won't agree with me, but I'm beginning to feel sorry for him. He wants to start a fight with you because you struck out his pa at the school softball game. He is sticking up for his pa, yet his pa doesn't treat Amos very well, from what you've said in your letters. I've decided that Amos is a very angry young man, and you are an easy target for him.

You did the right thing by not fighting with him, even when he started it. It was smart of you to move aside so he fell in the water. I kind of chuckled when you described it. I'll bet he made a big splash. But I suppose now he will be angrier than ever. I'm sure you'll let me know if Amos causes you any more problems.

The Struckmeyer Stupendous Family Circus: what a great name. I can't wait to hear more about it.

Love,
Grandma S.

June 19, 1938
Sunday

Dear Grandma,

I'm sorry it's been so long since my last letter, but I have been very busy working on a project. Today was Father's Day, and I really surprised Pa. I gave him a present he didn't expect.

Pa's old billfold isn't really a billfold at all, but a ratty little leather bag. It's almost worn through, and one day I heard Ma say to Pa, "Adolph, you're gonna lose the little money you've got if you keep it in that old money bag." Pa said it was all he had. I know Pa doesn't have any money to buy a new billfold. He'd probably buy a new halter for one of the horses before he'd buy a new billfold.

I wanted to make him a billfold with the leather tools that you gave me. Pa said he liked the looks of my billfold when he first saw it. And I told you about how even Amos Woodward likes my leatherwork—at school I caught him looking at my belt and all its little designs. When I brought in my billfold to show it to Miss Harvey and the other kids, he held it longer than anybody else when she passed it around. But since I have made a billfold and leather belt for myself, I didn't have any leather left to make something for Pa.

Last Saturday night I asked Pa if I could go off by myself while he went down to Johnson's Hardware store to talk with the other farmers. He assumed I was going to the drugstore for an ice cream cone like I usually do, and I didn't let him think anything different. But instead of going to the drugstore, I stopped at Wheeler's Harness Shop, a couple of doors farther down Main Street. I could smell new leather and harness oil as I walked in the door, which has a little bell attached to it. A man was working at a huge black sewing machine on a wooden counter.

"What can I do for you, young feller?" he asked me in a friendly voice.

"Are you Mr. Wheeler?" I asked.

"I am. And you are?" he said. I told him my name.

"You're Adolph's son, aren't you? I fixed one of your Pa's bridles a few weeks ago," Mr. Wheeler said. He stood up from his sewing machine, and I saw that he was wearing a long leather apron that came clear up under his whiskered chin and went well below his knees. He grabbed a badly worn wooden crutch that I hadn't seen standing in the corner and tucked it under his right arm.

"Got a bad leg," Mr. Wheeler said, when he noticed me watching. "Horses ran away from me when I was a kid, and the leg never healed right."

"I've got a bad leg, too," I blurted out. "Broke it when I fell out of a tree when we lived in Ohio."

"Don't look too bad," Mr. Wheeler said. He pushed his gold-rimmed glasses back on his nose. I told him my leg has been feeling a little better, but I still can't run. He said he can't run, either, and he held up his crutch and waved it around a little. Then he chuckled and asked how he could help me. I explained that I know something about making things from leather. I showed him my belt and my billfold and said I wanted to make a billfold for Pa for Father's Day, but I didn't have any leather.

"No leather, huh?" Mr. Wheeler said. He was studying my billfold pretty closely, running his thick, callused fingers over the designs and opening and closing it. He must have seen that I didn't have any money inside it. I asked Mr. Wheeler if he had leather for sale, and he said he did.

"Problem is," he said, "you've got no money. Nobody's got any money these days. Times better get better soon, or we'll all go broke." He was quiet for a minute, and then he asked me, "You really made this billfold?" I told him that I did and that I'd used tools my grandmother had given me. He asked me if you had shown me how to do leatherwork. Grandma, he was really impressed and said that you taught me well.

Mr. Wheeler turned and hobbled to the back of the harness shop, the crutch making a "clunk, clunk" sound as he walked. He returned carrying a hunk of new leather.

"I figure this piece of leather is big enough for two billfolds," he said. "You make one for your Pa and one for me to sell here in the shop, and the leather is yours."

I asked him if he was sure about that. He said he surely was. His blue eyes twinkled as he spoke, and a broad smile spread across his wrinkled face. I felt really good when he said, "I know good work when I see it. I expect to have my billfold finished in a couple weeks."

"You shall have it," I said.

I hurried to the car and tucked the brown package away on the back seat so Pa wouldn't see it. All week I spent every free minute I had working on the billfold. I even stamped Pa's initials, AS, on one side. I made a border all around the billfold that looks like little acorns all in a row. Then I made a tree design for the front. It really turned out great.

After we got back from church today, I handed Pa the package and said, "Happy Father's Day." He carefully untied the string and unwrapped the paper. Grandma, you should have seen the look on his face! He usually has something to say, but this time he just sat there, fingering the new leather billfold and even holding it up to his nose. Finally he said, "Thank you. I don't think I've gotten a nicer present."

It was a good day, Grandma. I sure am glad I got to meet Mr. Wheeler. Now I've got to get busy and finish the billfold that I owe him.

My circus is next Sunday afternoon. I hope somebody comes! I have put up my posters in Link Lake and nailed a few to trees along our road.

I hope you are enjoying summer.

Your grandson,
George

Dear George,

I wish I could have been there when you gave your pa a new billfold for Father's Day. What a fine idea that was, and what a nice man the harness maker in Link Lake must be to help you get the leather you needed. Your pa must be very proud of you. You and your pa seem to get along a lot better than Amos and his pa. I hope that with all you have going on in your life, you can keep finding time to work on your leather projects. It sounds like you've got to finish another billfold to complete the deal you made with the harness maker, and I'll bet you can work out other arrangements with him to sell your leather projects. I'm sure you've already thought of that.

How is the circus coming along?

Love,
Grandma S.

June 27, 1938
Monday

Dear Grandma,

We put on our circus yesterday, and I've got to tell you all about it. It was really fun, until near the end.

Here's how we set things up. The barn has a big open area with a huge door at one end where we haul in hay. I arranged some bales of straw there so people could sit while they watched the acts we had put together. On either side of this open area are wooden beams about fifteen feet from the floor. A rope hangs from the ceiling of the barn. Ordinarily we use it for pulling hay up into the barn.

Pa helped me clean up the upper part of the barn where we store hay. So far we have hauled only a few loads of hay into the barn, so it is mostly empty. But with that new hay up there, the inside of the barn sure smelled fresh and clean. Ma helped me make a big sign that we hung over the barn door that read: Struckmeyer Stupendous Family Circus. It was impressive.

I was surprised at how many people came to the circus. I counted twenty-five! They were mostly kids, but a few of the parents came along as well. Most were kids I know from school, but a few came all the way from Link Lake.

I charged one penny for admission. Just inside the barn door I had lined up a row of overturned potato crates with animals inside. Nearby I hung up a sign that read, "Menagerie." A potato crate has plenty of space between the slats, so it was easy to see what was in each crate. Under the first one I had put one of Ma's laying hens. On a little sign I had written: "Exotic Fowl from the Deeper Regions of Africa." I heard one kid say, "Looks like an ordinary chicken to me," but I didn't say anything. Under the second crate, I put one of our barn cats. That sign read, "Ferocious Feline from the Mountain Regions of the Andes." I picked one of our meanest barn cats, so if a kid got too close to the crate, it would snarl and show its claws. That old cat proved to be a wonderful actor.

Next up was a garter snake I found near the barn, a little one about six inches long. I put it in a shoe box with some grass and covered it with a little piece of window screen so the snake couldn't escape. The sign read, "Anaconda Snake from the Wilds of the Amazon. Known to Crush its Victims to Death." After reading the sign, most of the kids wouldn't even look in the box.

Under the next two overturned potato crates were two English sparrows that Pa helped me catch. The sign read, "Rare Avian Specimens from Deep within the Jungles of Central America."

Depot was the last exhibit in the menagerie. I made a little leather collar for him and tied him to a board in the barn with a sign that read, "The Most Dangerous of All the Lion Species Known to Man." I had to remind Annie that she shouldn't pet Depot, or the kids wouldn't believe the sign.

After everyone had a chance to see my wild animal collection, I crawled up on a pile of hay and in a loud voice said, "Ladies and gentlemen, children of all ages, welcome to the first performance of the Struckmeyer Stupendous Family Circus." Everyone took seats on the straw bales. The audience clapped as Annie rode into the barn on Ginger's back. Ma had dressed her in a frilly little red dress, and I had taught her how to hold on to the reins with one hand and wave with the other. Annie was smiling her biggest smile.

When Ginger heard all the clapping and the cheering, he must have remembered his circus days, because he held his head high and pranced all around the barn. Next came Rachel, with Gregory draped over her shoulders. I heard one kid whisper, "Is that animal real?" Just then Gregory lifted his head, and the youngster had his answer.

Annie slid off Ginger's back and handed the reins to me, and I put Ginger through his paces. He stood on his hind legs, knelt down, lay down, and played dead. I have taught him how to count by stamping one foot when I call out a number. (The key to the trick is for me to gently tap him on the leg the same number of times as the number I call out.) That trick was a real hit with the crowd. Ginger is clearly a star performer.

Next it was Gregory's turn. Rachel had placed a little leather collar around his neck, with a short leash attached. She put Gregory on the floor, and he sniffed and looked around at the kids as they clapped and cheered. Next she put a little covered can in front of the raccoon. He looked at it and then used his front paws to lift the cover off the can. Everyone cheered again. Rachel put a little bowl of water on the floor in front of Gregory. I'm sure the kids thought she was giving him a drink. Instead he lifted the bowl of water with both paws and turned it over, dumping the water on the floor. The kids just howled with laughter.

I had saved my aerial act for last. For the past several weeks, I have been practicing climbing up a ladder to one of the big beams, grabbing the rope that we use to pull hay into the barn, and swinging across an open area to another beam. I've gotten pretty good at it.

I climbed up the ladder, forgetting entirely about my bum leg. I grabbed the rope with one hand and waved to the audience fifteen feet below me, just like the aerialists did in the Ringling Brothers Circus. Then I grabbed the rope with both hands, pushed off, and sailed across the open area, landing on the opposite beam with no difficulty at all.

The audience loved it. They all clapped and cheered as I readied myself to swing back to the beam where I'd started. Both Pa and Ma were watching, and I must say, they looked a little concerned. I saw Ma hold her hand to her mouth when I grabbed the rope.

I hadn't noticed that Amos Woodward had arrived late, but all of a sudden there he was, glaring up at me. I took a sturdy grip on the rope and pushed off. But as I swung across the open area, Amos grabbed the end of the rope and stopped me from completing my swing to the opposite beam. I was stuck hanging above the audience. I didn't know what to do. The kids all scattered, not wanting me to fall on them. Amos held on to the rope, smirking at the scared look on my face. I saw Pa get up from his seat when he saw what Amos was doing. Amos let go of the rope, but there I hung, fifteen feet above the floor. No one said a word. After a few seconds my arms grew tired, and I let go of the rope. I landed with a big swoosh in a pile of hay, which cushioned my fall. I saw Amos stomping out of the barn just as I stood up, brushed the hay off my clothes, and waved. Everyone clapped and cheered.

I thanked everyone for coming and invited them to try some of Annie's lemonade, which she was selling for a penny a cup. (Ma helped her make it.)

We put on quite a show, Grandma. I hope the stunt Amos pulled didn't spoil it.

Your grandson,
George

Dear George,

Oh, what a great circus you put together, complete with "wild" animals! From what you described, Ginger stole the show, but didn't you expect him to? After all, he was a circus performer at one time. That raccoon, Gregory, is no slouch, either. It was nice of you to invite Rachel Williams to participate, and I'm so glad you involved your little sister, too. I'll bet she had lots of fun being a part of the show.

Swinging with a rope from the high beams in your barn—that really must have been something. Were you scared? I'll bet you could have heard a pin drop when you were doing that.

You are wondering if Amos spoiled the show. Believe me when I assure you that he didn't. Children know when they've seen something they like, and his little stunt didn't spoil it for them. I know you are disappointed that everything wasn't perfect. Think about what went right, and how your audience clapped and cheered. You did a good thing, bringing laughter and joy to people during these hard times.

Much love,
Grandma S.

June 28, 1938
Tuesday

Dear Grandma,

I'm still thinking about how much fun I had with my little circus, despite Amos's attempt to ruin my aerial act. I think everyone who came had a good time as well—they said they did, anyway. I was kind of tired yesterday, but I feel better today. Ginger doesn't seem his old self, though. I was so impressed with what he did and how he did it. But today all he wants to do is rest in his stall. I wonder if he overdid it?

Pa started making hay last week. He says the hay crop looks good, and he hopes it will be enough to last the cows and horses through the winter.

He hitched Maud and Tony to the hay mower, and soon it was chattering around the hayfield, cutting off the alfalfa, clover, and timothy (that's what Pa said grows in the field). By noontime, he had half of one field cut. He left the hay to dry in the field. Drying hay smells so good. I can't say I've ever smelled anything like it.

Late that afternoon Pa finished cutting the field and started raking the hay. Our hay rake is something to see. It has two high, narrow wheels, and between them is a row of steel tines that look like half circles. Pat sits on a high seat in the middle and pushes a lever with his foot every so often, leaving the raked hay in a ropelike row across the field. The rake must be easy to pull, because the horses really high-stepped their way around the field, swinging their tails. Before you knew it, Pa had ropes of hay strung all across the field.

Pa said my job was to pile the ropes of hay into little stacks, which are called hay bunches. I used a three-tine fork to gather the hay and make hay bunches about as tall as I am.

Pa says, "If you're a good farmer, your hay bunches won't tip over." I haven't decided whether I want to be a good farmer—or whether I want to be any kind of farmer. But I tried to do the best I could. If a hay bunch tips over, the hay will get wet when it rains and will spoil. Pretty soon I had hay bunches sprinkled all over the hayfield. This is the kind of work where you can see the results right away.

The next morning, after the dew was off and the hay had a chance to dry some more, Pa finished raking and then he helped me make hay bunches. Soon the field was finished—hay bunches everywhere. On the hilltops. In the hollows. Along the fencerows. Pa said that if the sun kept shining and the breezes kept blowing, we could haul the hay to the barn the next day. And that's what we did. But something happened that we didn't expect.

Remember the old steel-wheeled wagon that I used to haul seed oats home from the neighbors'? Well, we lifted the box off the wagon and replaced it with a hayrack. The hayrack is three times as wide as the wagon box—so there is room in it for lots of hay—and it has a tall wooden framework on each end to keep the hay from falling off the wagon once it is loaded.

My job was to drive the wagon in the field and move the hay around on the hayrack as Pa pitched the hay bunches up to me. He's good at pitching hay and can toss an entire hay bunch on the wagon with one throw. As the load of hay got higher and higher, far above his head, he continued tossing up hay bunches, until I was a little befuddled about how to keep the load even so it wouldn't tip over. Pa kept telling me, "I think you need a little more here" or "You need a little more there," pointing to places where he figured the load needed a little help.

When the load was finished, he crawled up on the wagon with me and we slowly drove across the rough hayfield to the barn. I could see Maud and Tony leaning into their harnesses, sweat soaking them as they plodded toward the barn.

At the barn Pa drove the load of hay onto what he calls the threshing floor, a place where earlier farmers threshed their grain by hand. Pa unhitched

Maud, led her out of the barn, and hitched her to the end of a long, heavy rope that is threaded through a series of pulleys to the hay storage areas in the barn. Pa calls these storage areas haymows. (The word "mow" rhymes with "cow" and "now.") Pa crawled up on the wagon and pushed a hayfork—a tool with two steel prongs about three feet long—into the load of hay. Then he yelled, "Ready!"

I said "giddap" to Maud, and as she moved slowly forward, the big rope tightened, the pulleys squeaked, and a huge hunk of hay lifted from the wagon as Pa stood clear, watching it. When the hayfork reached the metal track in the ceiling of the barn, it rolled along above one of the haymows. Just as it was at the middle of the haymow, Pa yelled, "Whoa," and I pulled on the lines to stop Maud. Pa pulled a smaller rope, called a trip rope, and the hay dropped with a "whoosh" and a cloud of dust and hay leaves.

We did this over and over, until the hay wagon was bare. Then both Pa and I climbed into the haymow and began forking the hay into every nook and cranny of the barn. What a job. And was it hot! It must have been more than a hundred degrees up under the roof of the barn. Walking on loose hay, where you sink well above your knees, doesn't make the job any easier. It's about the hardest work on the farm. The good smell of the fresh hay didn't make up for the hard work, and we are just getting started with the haying season. Pa told me that by the time we finish haying, the haymows will be filled with hay clear to the hayfork track.

Then the unexpected thing happened. We were working on the second load of hay. Pa was pitching hay onto the wagon, while I was driving the team from hay bunch to hay bunch and arranging the hay on the wagon. (Pa calls this "making a load.") I wasn't paying much attention to Pa other than trying to stay ahead of him, when I heard him yell. I looked up and saw that he had dropped his three-tine fork and was running across the field, swinging his straw hat around his head, yelling, "Bees, bees!" At the time it was rather comical. I have never seen Pa run faster, not even when he was playing ball at the end-of-school-year picnic.

The next thing I knew, Pa had stuck his head into a hay bunch. He stayed there for a little while, but eventually he came walking back to wagon, rubbing his neck. His face and hair were covered with hay leaves.

"Look at you," I chuckled.

"Bees got me," he said. He continued rubbing his neck, which I could see was swelling. "Gotta put something on these stings," he said.

I helped him onto the wagon, and I drove home. Pa sat quietly all the way home, holding his head in his hands. When we got to the house, I tied the team to a tree near the kitchen and ran to tell Ma what happened. Somewhere she learned that bread soaked in milk is a good treatment for beestings, and she quickly prepared a mixture, which she called a poultice. In the meantime, Pa sat on the porch in a kind of daze.

Ma was concerned when she looked at all the beestings on Pa's neck. She put the bread and milk poultice in place and tied a dish towel over the concoction. Then she helped Pa walk into the house and over to the couch in the dining room. Pa said that

Ma and I should unload the hay and put the horses away, because we wouldn't be hauling any more hay that day.

I tried to do what Pa had done, while Ma drove Maud on the hayfork rope. Between the two of us, we managed to unload the partial load of hay. I left forking the hay around in the mow for another day. I unharnessed the horses and turned them out in the barnyard.

When I got back in the house, I saw that Pa's neck was swelled to twice its normal size and his face was a sickly red. Ma was worried. She was on the phone to Grandma Woodward, asking what she could do besides the bread and milk poultice. Grandma Woodward told Ma how to mix a concoction that would make Pa sick when he drank it and take the bee poison from his system.

Ma and I milked the cows, and Annie helped us feed the calves. I surprised myself with how much I can do, even with my gimpy leg.

I heard Pa throwing up most of the night. In the morning when I looked in on him, he was as pale as bread flour, but the swelling had gone down.

"Afraid you and Ma will have to do the milking again this morning," he said. "I can barely stand up, I'm so weak."

"You're lucky you're alive," Ma said. "Grandma Woodward told me she had heard of people dying with fewer beestings than you had."

It took a couple of days before Pa was back to his old self and we could continue haying. He gave us quite a scare. I didn't know that beestings could be so dangerous. I also learned that when someone is sick, you have to take up the slack, as the farm work still needs doing.

Your grandson,
George

July 4, 1938
Monday

Dear Grandma,

We are still making hay. The barn is nearly filled, but still I wonder if we'll ever finish. I don't want to see another load of hay for the rest of my life. And I'll bet Maud and Tony feel the same way. Pa and I are out in the field every day, making hay bunches, loading them on the wagon, and forking the hay around in the haymow. Hay doesn't smell nearly as good as it did when we first started; now it smells like work. Hard, sweaty, never-ending, day-after-day work.

I've been learning how to use a three-tine fork. Haying is easier if you know where to grab the fork handle, know how to twist it, and know when to push and when to pull. Don't laugh, Grandma. All these things make a difference. If you use the fork right, you finish the day a little less tired. Like Pa always says, "Little things make the difference." He's sure right when it comes to a three-tine fork.

At the breakfast table this morning, Pa said it was the Fourth of July and that we would work only

122

until noon. He said we would drive to Round Lake, where there's a big community celebration, and he asked Ma if she would pack a picnic dinner.

I spent the morning making hay bunches, thinking about Round Lake and the Fourth of July celebration. Pa had said there would be games for the little kids to play, like drop the handkerchief and blind man's bluff. I knew Annie would have fun playing those. A few days ago when we were at the mill waiting for cow feed to be ground, Pa and I heard that the celebration would include a big tug-of-war between the older kids. I hoped that I might be a part of that. It's done over a small pond, so participants are told to bring along a change of clothes in case they fall into the water.

Ma made her special potato salad, a chocolate cake, and a batch of beans and packed it all up with some sandwiches. She even stirred up a jar of lemonade with slices of yellow lemons floating on top. We all climbed into the car and were off to Round Lake for dinner and an afternoon of fun. Even though the outing was Pa's idea, I suspect he was worried about the hay that was sitting out in the field. But I figured a half day away from it surely wouldn't hurt anything, unless we got a pouring rain, but it didn't look like any rain was coming anytime soon.

It seemed like everyone in the world was at Round Lake. We could hardly find a place to park the car. Kids were running around, swinging and sliding down the metal slides, and swimming. Families were spreading tablecloths on picnic tables and getting ready to eat. I think we got one of the last tables in the shade, under a big old pine tree.

While Ma spread out the meal, I walked over

to a bulletin board, where a sign said that everyone interested in the tug-of-war should gather near the lake at two o'clock.

Ma called out that dinner was ready. I sat down, and we dug into one of the best meals I've ever eaten. Maybe that's because I don't get potato salad, baked beans, and chocolate cake every day. Or maybe it's because I worked up a powerful hunger making hay for the last three weeks. Either way, I ate way too much, and after I was finished I mostly wanted to crawl off in the shade and take a nap.

Pa shook me. He was holding his pocket watch in his hand.

"Five minutes to two," he said. "Didn't you want to try the tug of war?"

I got up and made my way toward the shore of the lake, where a large crowd had gathered. A tall man with a big voice was announcing, "Everybody interested in the tug-of-war, assemble right here." Ma, Pa, and Annie walked over to the tug-of-war area, too, to watch the contest.

Wouldn't you know it, Grandma? When I lined up for the tug-of-war, the first person I saw was Amos Woodward.

"What're you doin' here, Struckmeyer?" he growled at me. "This game's for strong kids, not ones with gimpy legs."

"If you can do it, I can do it," I told him.

"Here, here, boys!" the announcer said. He was wearing a little flat-topped straw hat with a red band around it. "Everybody who wants to play can. I think I'll put you boys on opposite sides. Might be interesting."

He pointed to where each of us should stand. We were on opposite sides of a little pond of murky water that someone had dug in the sand next to the lake. The pond was about six feet across by four feet wide. I couldn't tell how deep it was because the water was so cloudy. A piece of hayfork rope, maybe thirty feet long, lay across the pond.

Soon the tall fellow with the straw hat had us all organized. I suspect he was counting us to make sure each side had the same number of kids. I wished he had paid more attention to the size of the kids. I glanced across the pond and saw a bunch of big strong farm kids.

"Here are the rules," the announcer began. "When I shoot this gun, start pulling." He pulled a pistol with a white handle out of his pocket. (It looked like a real gun to me, but later Pa told me that it shot blank cartridges.)

"The idea is to pull the other side into this here pond. The winning team does it two out of three times. Is everybody ready?"

I grabbed hold of the rope with all my might.

"Kaboom!" The pistol shot echoed across the lake. I hadn't expected it to be so loud and dang near fell down when it went off.

Grandma, before I knew it, I was dragged right to the edge of that little muddy pond. I saw Amos on the other side grinning like crazy, his face getting redder by the second as he pulled on the rope. I planted my good leg in the sand, yelled over my shoulder, "Pull!" and, by golly, slowly my team eased away from the pond's edge. Of course this meant that Amos was getting that much closer to the pond.

I looked up to see that his face was even redder than before, and now his smile was gone. "Pull! Pull!" he yelled.

I was so proud of my team, Grandma. I didn't even know most of the kids, because they came from all around Link Lake, but we sure knew how to pull together. The next thing I knew, Amos had toppled into the pond of muddy water, followed by one teammate after the other. It was hilarious to see a pond full of kids all wet and muddy and tangled up in the hayfork rope.

"Kaboom!" The pistol shot stopped the pulling.

"Favor to this team," the thin man said, pointing at us. A big yell went up from my team as we watched the other kids crawl out of the pond, dripping with water and mud.

"For the next go, we switch sides," the tall man said. We ran around to the other side.

"I'll get you this time," Amos said as he walked past. He was a mess—mud on his pants, on his shirt, on his face, in his hair.

Now we had a wet rope to deal with, and before you could say, "You're gonna get muddy and wet," my team was in the pond.

So there we were, two teams of wet, muddy kids, with a rope that was wet on both ends, and one more pull to decide the winner.

The announcer had us switch sides once more and said, "This time whoever pulls the other team into the water wins."

I looked around at my teammates. What a wet mess we were, with mud in our hair, covering our clothing, everywhere. The same went for Amos's team. Each side grabbed the muddy rope and began pulling and pulling. First one side was on the brink of tumbling into the pond, then the other. Finally, Amos pulled a dirty trick. He said quietly so the judge couldn't hear, "We give up." Of course, he didn't mean it. But several of the kids on my team quit pulling. The minute they did, Amos and his team gave a mighty yank, and everyone on my team fell in the muddy pond once more. We lost the tug-of-war.

Pa was laughing when I crawled out of the muddy pond the second time. I was soaked to the skin.

I stripped off my shirt, shoes, and socks and jumped into the lake, wearing only my muddy pants. Eventually I was clean enough to crawl into the dry clothes I had brought along.

I walked by Amos on my way to the car. "Told you I'd get you," Amos said. He had a snarly look on his face. I didn't say anything. Why does he have to be this way, Grandma? I didn't mind being wet and muddy—or even losing the contest. But Amos cheated. Pa has taught me never to cheat, no matter what.

Your grandson,
George

Dear George,

We have had a string of hot, hot days here in Cleveland. I wish I could spend a few days at your farm, but I just can't afford a long trip right now. I'll bet it is cooler there in the country, away from all the big buildings.

Your father's encounter with the bees sounds dreadful. Beestings can be dangerous. But I don't have to tell you that—you saw it firsthand. I'm very glad he's feeling better now.

What a Fourth of July celebration! Picnics are fun, aren't they? And having one near a lake makes it even more fun.

Amos Woodward just doesn't give up, does he? I would have liked to have seen his face when your tug-of-war team pulled his team into the muddy water. It seems you didn't mind getting wet and dirty—it's part of the fun, isn't it? Who cares if you win or lose? It's having fun while you're doing something that counts. At least, that's what I've always thought. But I can understand your disappointment over Amos cheating. It's no fun competing with someone who cheats.

I'm looking forward to some cooler weather.

Much love,
Grandma S.

July 12, 1938
Tuesday

Dear Grandma,

It was an awful day, Grandma. Just awful. Remember that I told you that Ginger didn't feel well after he performed so well in the circus? This morning, Depot and

I went over to his stall to say good morning to him, as we do every morning, and I noticed that he was lying down, with his head stretched out in front on him. Pa was there with a glum look on his face. I reached out to pet Ginger, and his neck was cold.

"He's dead," Pa said in a quiet voice. "Likely had a heart attack. He was pretty old, you know."

I burst into tears. Depot put his nose close to Ginger's head and let out a high-pitched bark. It was a mournful sound. Ginger and Depot had become good buddies, and Ginger was gone.

Pa blew his nose into his handkerchief and then said, "Well, the cows still need to be milked. After breakfast we'll bury Ginger."

Grandma, I milked cows this morning with tears running down my face and dripping into the milk pail. I wonder if anyone will notice that their milk tastes salty.

Breakfast was a quiet affair. When little Annie heard about Ginger, she began sobbing and didn't quit. She wouldn't eat breakfast. I didn't eat very much. All I could think about was Ginger lying dead in the barn. No more circus performances, no good times riding him around the yard, no more circus tricks.

We buried Ginger on the hill on the west side of the farm, next to some big pine trees. When we finished, Pa cut a couple of pine tree branches and used some twine to fashion a cross. He pushed it into the ground at one end of the grave. Ma, Annie, and Depot were there with us. Annie put some wildflowers on the grave next to the cross. Ma had picked a couple of roses from the rosebush that grows alongside our house, and she gently placed them on Ginger's grave as well. Then we all stood there with our heads bowed. Pa asked if I'd like to say some words over the grave. "Ginger was a good pony," was all I could think to say. And then I started crying and mumbled, "Why did you have to die?"

Pa put his hand on my shoulder. He said, "George, remember what I told you when Polly died? On a farm there is birth, and there is death. One we look forward to, and the other we don't. But both happen. And we must go on." He took out his handkerchief and blew his nose. I could see tears in his eyes. Ma was crying, too, and Annie was sobbing with her head buried in Ma's apron.

Pa turned to walk back to the house, and the rest of us followed, all except Depot. He lay on Ginger's grave, and as we left he lifted his head and howled a long, deep sound that I've never heard him make before. He stayed at Ginger's grave all day, finally coming home when it was getting dark.

This evening around the supper table we were very quiet. Then Pa said, "Let's each say something we remember about Ginger." And that's what we did. I told about how well he had performed in the Struckmeyer Family Circus. Annie talked about how much fun she had had riding him. Ma said she just liked having him around and that he was such a friendly little pony. Pa said he thought Ginger was always smiling.

It will be hard to not keep thinking about Ginger, Grandma.

Love,
George

Dear George,

I'm so very sorry to hear about Ginger. What a wonderful little pony he was. I wish I could have gotten to know him. I know how bad you and your family must be feeling. Ginger had become a part of your family, too.

Try to remember the good times you had with him and feel good that you and your family took such good care of him after he came to your farm. Remember, too, that you gave him one last chance to perform in front of a crowd of people. From what you wrote, that was something Ginger really enjoyed doing.

I'm sorry, George. There's nothing more I can say.

Love,
Grandma S.

July 15, 1938
Friday

Dear Grandma,

Today is my thirteenth birthday. I hadn't heard Ma or Pa say one thing about it, and I was sure they had forgotten. I know there is no money for presents. And since we are just winding up the haying season, there is still plenty of work to do and no time for celebrations.

When I got up at five-thirty this morning, I was still thinking about Ginger, and, I must say, feeling pretty sorry for myself. I limped out to the barn to milk my cows as usual. Pa didn't say anything other than "Good morning, George," which he says every morning when I open the barn door. No mention of my birthday. Just some comment about it being a nice day for making hay. The last thing I wanted to hear about was making hay. That's about all we've done for the past month.

Nothing was different at breakfast, either. Ma made oatmeal, fried eggs with bacon, and sliced hunks of homemade bread spread with butter and homemade strawberry jam. The usual. Nobody had much to say while we ate. Annie finished her breakfast and went off to play.

"Something wrong?" Ma asked when she noticed I was dawdling over my oatmeal.

"Nothing wrong, Ma," I answered. But there was something wrong—mighty wrong. Here it was my birthday, and nobody had even mentioned it. When I finished eating, I started to get up from the table, but Pa said, "Why don't you wait a minute?"

Just then Annie came through the door from the dining room carrying a pile of packages that came almost up to her chin. She was smiling the biggest smile I've ever seen. "Happy birthday!" everyone said.

I was absolutely speechless. Annie started handing me packages.

"This one is from me," she said. "Open it." I tore open the paper and found a big red handkerchief, the kind Pa uses.

I thanked her and opened the next package. I found a new shirt from Ma. Your package was in the pile, too, Grandma. Thank you so much for the new supply of writing paper and the new pencils, too. I also liked your card.

The biggest surprise came from Pa. There was one tiny package left. I had no idea what it could be. I shook the package, but it made not a sound.

I ripped off the paper and inside found a plain brown box. I lifted the cover, and there was a beautiful new jackknife with a bone handle and three blades.

"You're old enough to have your own knife," Pa told me.

"Thank you," I said. I had all I could do to keep from crying. Grandma, there's nothing I've been wanting more than a knife. I've been eyeing the collection of knives in the glass-covered display case at Johnson's Hardware. Johnson's has everything from tiny penknives to huge hunting knives that you carry on your hip in a leather sheath. Now I have my very own jackknife for whittling, cutting string, working with leather—doing all the jobs that require a knife.

"Take care of it, George, and that knife will last a lifetime." Pa said. He had a big grin on his face. I told him I surely will.

Then he really surprised me. "One more present, George: no work for you today. You can do whatever you want—read, work with your leather, anything. It's your day." I just about fell off my chair.

The first thing I did was hike up to Ginger's grave, where I placed a couple roses from Ma's rosebush. Depot went with me, of course. I sat under the big pine tree near the grave and listened to the wind move through the pine needles and breathed in the fresh smell of pine. Depot lay with his head on the grave. I thought about Ginger and all the good times we had together. I sat there most of the day. I had brought along one of my books, so I read a little, and I even took a little nap under the trees where the fallen pine needles have made a soft bed. Depot lay down beside me and napped, too.

Ma had invited Grandma Woodward over after supper for birthday cake, and everyone sang "Happy Birthday" after I blew out the thirteen candles with one big puff.

It was the best birthday I've ever had.

Your grandson,
George

July 20, 1938
Wednesday

Dear Grandma,

I heard the rumble of thunder during the night and woke up once to see my room as bright as daylight as lightning flashed. At five-thirty, when it was time to get up, rain was still dripping off the roof and splashing against my bedroom window. I heard the thunder growl, but it wasn't as close as it was during the night.

The cows dripped rainwater when Pa let them into the barn for milking. The smell of wet cowhide is something I can do without, but it's a part of milking cows on a rainy morning.

"Looks like a good day for fishing," Pa said. It was too wet to work in our fields.

By the time we finished milking and turned the cows back out to pasture, the rain had slowed to a mist. Pa and I dug earthworms back of the chicken house. (We use earthworms for bait.) We found our long cane fishing poles and the fish hooks that Pa buys at Johnson's Hardware, and we headed for Church Lake, which is just down the hill from the Norwegian church. I have seen fish jumping nearly every Sunday morning when we attend church. Now I was hoping to hook one.

Pa parked the car in the church lot, and we walked down to the lake. He lugged the fishing poles, while I carried the can of earthworms and the lunch Ma had made for us. Depot came along, too, and bounced along beside me. He is hardly a puppy anymore, he has grown so much this summer.

Church Lake is not real big but not tiny, either. I suspect a good ball player could throw a ball across the narrowest part of the lake. It has several little coves that by this time of the summer are filled with pond lilies. Pa says these are good places to catch fish, as the fish like to hide under the lilies, where it's a little cooler and where they can find plenty to eat.

We unwound the line from our fishing poles, tied on cork bobbers, threaded fat worms on our hooks, and tossed out. The surface of the lake was so smooth it looked like you could walk on it. I saw a long-legged bird standing in the water near the opposite shore. Pa said it was a great blue heron and that it is better at fishing than we are. I watched the heron standing there like a statue, and then all of a sudden it slammed its bill into the water and came up with a fish. Just then my cork began jumping a little—not going under, just dipping up and down.

"You're getting a bite," Pa said. "When it goes under, pull up your pole."

I noticed that Depot was watching my bobber as well, his head cocked to the side. I tightened my grip on the pole and watched. Dip, dip, dip, then gone. I lifted my long cane pole. I had snagged a big bluegill, and soon I had it flopping on the shore, the hook caught in its lip. Depot tried to catch the flopping bluegill but didn't succeed. It was quite a sight: the fish flopping, and Depot jumping around after it. I grabbed Depot by his collar and asked Pa to hold him while I removed the hook from the bluegill's lip. Then I shoved the fish into the old burlap bag Pa had brought along, and Pa tied the top shut and put it in the water close to shore. He explained that this would keep the fish alive as long as possible and keep the meat fresh.

Soon both of us were catching bluegills one after the other. We stopped fishing at noon to eat our sandwiches and lay in the tall grass on the shore of the lake. A little breeze was blowing away the clouds and rippling the surface of the lake.

After our break we got back to fishing. Before long I could scarcely lift the wet bag of fish out of the lake to slip in another one.

"Got enough for a couple good meals," Pa said. "Let's fish for a few more minutes and then head home."

My bobber floated quietly, no action at all. No bites, no fish. "Nothing biting," I said. I had no more than said it when my bobber disappeared—no dancing on the water, no going under and then coming up again. It was just plain gone. I started lifting my pole, but I couldn't budge whatever was in the water, grabbing my bait.

I pulled harder, and then I heard a crack. The bottom three feet of my fishing pole broke off in my hands. I made a lunge for the rest of the pole and fell in the lake. I stumbled to my feet, wet and spitting water, but I still had hold of what remained of my broken cane pole. It was then that I noticed Depot in the water with me, paddling with all four legs.

"You all right, George?" Pa yelled.

"Yeah," I answered when I finally stopped coughing.

"Grab hold of the line," Pa yelled. I pulled the jerking pole through my hand until I got the line, which I pulled hand over hand. The line jerked and tugged, and once I thought I was going head first into the lake again. Depot somehow got tangled in the fish line as well. Slowly I struggled toward shore, dragging the line with one hand and trying to hold onto Depot with the other as I trudged through the ooze and the tangle of pond lilies. I was soaked from one end to the other.

"Here," Pa said. "Let me help you with the line."

Pa grabbed the line, and slowly we retrieved it, both wondering what was on the other end. Just then there was a terrific tug. I lost my grip, but Pa held on.

I crawled up on shore, pulling Depot with me. As I did, I saw Pa pull a giant northern pike out of the water. It flopped around on the shore, but this time a very wet Depot kept his distance.

"I bet this fish will go five pounds," Pa said. "Can't wait to weigh it."

We retrieved our sack of bluegills and headed home, where we weighed the fish on Pa's scale in the granary. "Quite a fish you got there. Weighs five and a half pounds," Pa said. "We'll ask Ma to bake it."

I had a chance to use my new jackknife when I helped Pa clean the fish. A jackknife sure comes in handy.

We had fresh fish for three days, Grandma. What a treat. Fried bluegills are tasty, but baked northern pike is even better.

I can't wait to go fishing again.

Your grandson,
George

August 10, 1938
Wednesday

Dear Grandma,

I knew it would happen, and it did. There wasn't much I could do about it, either. Amos made good on his threat.

We were threshing oats at Rachel Williams's farm when it happened. A week ago Pa had cut our oat crop, and we had stood the oat bundles into grain shocks. Our neighbors did the same thing. Now it was time to thresh the grain.

Threshing is different from anything else we do on the farm. It is a community event where all the neighbors go from farm to farm for what usually amounts to a day of threshing for each neighbor. Horse-drawn wagons go out into the oat field, where the driver loads grain bundles and hauls them to the threshing machine. A threshing machine is huge—three times bigger than our Plymouth car, maybe even bigger. It separates the oat seeds from the stems and blows the chaff and stems onto a straw pile.

On Tuesday I drove our team and hay wagon over to Rachel's farm. On the way I passed by Amos Woodward's place, a plain-looking farmstead with a long driveway and buildings that need paint. The road is dusty and crooked, with a couple of steep little hills. Maud and Tony didn't seem to mind as they walked along with me standing on the empty wagon.

I noticed three other wagons already working in the Williamses' oat field when I arrived, one of them driven by Amos. I made sure I worked on a side of the field as far away from his wagon as possible.

But Amos and I arrived at the threshing machine at the same time. He pulled his load to one side of the machine's feeder, and I pulled up to the other side. We scarcely exchanged glances. I could see several of the neighbors working around the machine; one was forking straw on the straw stack, and others were ready to carry the threshed grain to the granary.

"You guys ready?" Joe Carlson yelled. He owns and operates the thresher, and he was sitting on his big red tractor, ready to set things into motion.

I nodded, and so did Amos. The big threshing machine began shaking and shuddering. Its many belts started slowly turning, and the elevator that moves the bundles into the machine creaked into motion.

Amos forked a bundle onto the elevator, and I followed. Amos, then me. It was going well until Amos started forking bundles faster. I, of course, had to keep up. Soon both of us were working furiously, pitching bundles as fast as we could.

"What are you guys doin'?" yelled Mr. Carlson. But Amos didn't hear or didn't want to, and I figured I just had to keep up with Amos. Soon the threshing machine began to shudder and shake more violently, and then it growled to a stop.

"You guys oughta know better," Mr. Carlson yelled. "You've plugged the machine."

"It was George's idea," Amos yelled.

I wanted to yell back that Amos had started it, but I didn't say anything.

"Well, don't you ever do that again, either one of you," shouted Mr. Carlson. It took a half hour for him to finish unplugging the machine and get the threshing started again.

On our way to dinner, I asked Amos why he told everyone it was my idea to pitch bundles fast and plug the machine. He said, "'Cause I wanted to."

"You started it, and you know it," I said.

"You know that, and I know that, but Carlson and the rest of the men don't, now do they?" Amos said.

"You're mean," I blurted out.

"I'm tough," replied Amos, a sneer spreading across his tanned face. "You gotta be tough when you live in the country."

I said that I'm tough, too, but that's not the same thing as being mean. I told him, "You chose to be mean, and I kept up with you, too, until the machine plugged up and stopped." Amos went into the house for dinner ahead of me without saying another word.

After the noon break we were back hauling bundles and unloading them at the threshing machine. Amos and I didn't find ourselves paired at the machine again that day, which must have been good luck on my part.

I was tired at day's end and started the team home along the road. I sat on the edge of the wagon, not thinking about much of anything, when I heard a voice say, "How about a race?" Amos had pulled up behind me, his team at the trot. I told him I didn't want to race and that he should pull out and pass me. I drove Maud and Tony to the side of the gravel road so Amos would have enough room to go by.

When Amos got alongside my team, he took the end of his leather lines and brought them down across the rumps of Maud and Tony. They took off at a gallop, almost tossing me from the wagon.

"Hay ya!" Amos yelled at his team. They are a pair of western-type horses, smaller than Maud and Tony but no doubt faster.

For the first quarter mile or so, the two teams galloped side by side, thundering down the narrow, twisting road. I hauled on the lines, keeping Maud and Tony from running off the narrow road, or worse, crashing into Amos's wagon. A big cloud of dust poured up from behind us as the two teams and steel-wheeled wagons bounced down the road.

"Hay ya!" Amos yelled again. He swung the ends of the leather lines across the backsides of his team as they pounded down the road ever faster.

The road made a sharp turn at the bottom of a hill. I don't know if Amos's wagon couldn't make the turn or if one of the wheels broke, but his wagon rolled over, and Amos flew off into some raspberry bushes. When the wagon tipped, Amos's team stopped, their sides heaving and sweat pouring from them.

"Whoa, whoa!" I yelled to Maud and Tony, pulling on the lines to stop them. I had no more than stopped the team when I felt something yanking on my leg. It was Amos, blood streaking down his face from the raspberry thorns. He pulled me off the wagon and took a mighty swing at me. His thick fist caught me just below the eye, and I fell in the dusty road. Before I could stand up, Amos was on top of me, pounding with both of his hands. I swung at him and got in a couple of good licks.

Just then Pa came by in the car on his way home from Rachel's place. He saw us rolling in the dirt in the middle of the road. He stopped the car, ran out, and pulled us apart. "What has gotten into you two?" he said. "Can't you get along for one minute?"

I didn't say anything. Neither did Amos. Pa looked at Amos's wagon and at his team. "Busted up your wagon pretty good," he said to Amos as he helped him unhitch the horses. "George, you drive Maud and Tony home—and you better walk them." I could see that Pa was mad, and you never want to make Pa mad. I hoped he would cool off by the time I got home with the team.

As I started off down the road, Amos headed in

the other direction, walking along behind his team without the wagon. I wondered what his Pa was going to say to him.

When I got home, Pa helped me unhitch the team, unharness them, brush them down, and turn them out to pasture.

"Got yourself quite a shiner there," he said. He was looking at my black eye, which I hadn't yet seen but sure could feel. "Don't you ever run that team again," he said. "Ever."

"I won't," I said. I wanted to tell him what Amos had done, but I thought better of it. I don't think Pa was in the mood to hear any excuses. I'm surprised he didn't say anything about the fight. I expected a tongue-lashing about that, too.

I guess I've got a lifelong enemy, Grandma. My eye hurts like everything, but not as much as I hurt inside. I don't like having people mad at me.

Your grandson,
George

August 14, 1938
Sunday

Dear Grandma,

An awful thing happened yesterday. Depot and I were on our way to fetch the cows from the pasture when I caught a whiff of smoke. At first I thought maybe Ma had put a fresh stick of wood in the stove. But then I realized the wind was blowing in the wrong direction for me to smell smoke coming from our chimney.

I walked on toward the far side of the pasture where I thought I'd find the cows. When I got to the top of the ridge, I smelled smoke again, stronger this time. I think Depot smelled it too, as he held his head high and sniffed the air. It smelled different from burning oak or pine kindling, which is what Ma uses in our cook stove.

From up on the ridge I could see our house, and I could also see Grandma Woodward's little house in the distance. Then something stopped me cold. Smoke was pouring out of Grandma Woodward's kitchen door and out the kitchen windows, too. Grandma Woodward's house was on fire.

Her house was about a half mile from where I was standing. I didn't see any other people. I was the only one who knew her house was on fire. I started moving toward her house as fast as I could, Depot bounding along beside me. The faster I moved, the faster I discovered I *could* move. Soon I was running, forgetting that my gimpy leg was supposed to slow me down. I raced across the road and up her driveway, calling, "Grandma Woodward! Grandma Woodward!" No response. I ran up to the screen door and began pounding on it and yelling, "Grandma Woodward!"

The smoke pouring through the screen door was so thick I could see inside only a few feet. "Are you in there, Grandma Woodward?" I yelled again. I could see flames licking at the curtains and running up the kitchen wall. I jerked on the screen door, but it was hooked from inside and wouldn't open. Then I remembered my new jackknife. I took it out of my pocket and opened the big blade. Smoke was stinging my eyes and I began coughing.

I cut a hole in the thin wire screen large enough so I could push my hand through and unhook the door. All the while I kept calling, "Grandma Woodward!" Grandma Woodward!"

The smoke was less thick near the floor, so I got on my knees and began crawling across the kitchen floor. Depot stayed outside, barking like crazy. I had crawled only a few feet when I bumped into something soft. It was Grandma Woodward, lying on her stomach with her hands over her head. I shook her and called her name, but she didn't respond. She didn't even open her eyes.

I put my hands under her arms and dragged her toward the door. Slowly I made my way through the smoke. Now the flames were crawling along the ceiling above the stove.

When I finally got to the door with Grandma Woodward, my eyes hurt so much I could hardly see. I was coughing so hard I had trouble pulling her. But I lugged her through the door and onto the porch. Trying to be careful, I pulled her out onto the lawn, several feet away from the burning house. Depot lay down next to her and licked her face. I fell over on my back, trying to catch my breath and focus my smoke-filled eyes.

"George, George, you all right?" It was Pa. Behind him were Amos Woodward and his pa. I could see tears streaming down Amos's face as he put a handkerchief on Grandma Woodward's forehead.

He had wet it at the pump. Grandma Woodward was moaning and coughing, but color was starting to return to her face.

By this time a dozen or more neighbors had arrived. They began throwing pails of water on the fire. Ma had noticed the fire about the same time I did, and she had called telephone central to put out a general ring on the party line phone. The general ring had summoned neighbors from miles away. One came with a pickup truck filled with cans of water. Another placed a ladder against the house so the roof could be soaked with water. Others went into the smoky kitchen and doused the flames with pails of water. Within a few minutes the kitchen fire was out, and Grandma Woodward was sitting up, concerned that so many people were fussing over her.

"You feeling better, Grandma?" Amos asked. I noticed that he had slipped his jacket under her head for a pillow.

"My gosh, yes. I must have passed out." she said. She sounded confused.

"The smoke got ya, Grandma," Amos said.

"Mercy me, I do remember that old apron falling on the stove and catching fire," she said. Her voice was raspy. "I thought I could put it out, but I guess I didn't. Trying to do a little canning today. Sweet corn is ready, you know."

"You gotta take it easy for a while, Grandma," Amos said. "You could have died in there."

"Mercy me. Mercy me," she said.

I was feeling better, too. I had stopped coughing, and my eyes had quit stinging. Depot seemed okay, too.

Pa was telling the neighbors about how I had dragged Grandma Woodward out of the house just as he, Amos, and Amos's pa arrived on the scene. Some of them came over to me and patted me on the back, telling me I had done a good thing. Others were petting Depot.

"Couldn't have done it without my jackknife," I said, holding it up so everyone could see.

When everything had quieted down and it had been decided that Grandma Woodward will stay with Amos and his family until her house is repaired, Amos came up to me, holding his hat in his hand. "George," he said quietly. I saw that his face was dirty and streaked with tears.

"Yes, Amos?" I said, not knowing what to expect.

"Thanks for saving my grandma."

"It's okay," I said. "I like her, too."

"Could I have a look at your jackknife?" Amos asked.

"Sure." I pulled it back out of my pocket and handed it to him.

"Nice knife," he said. He handed it back to me.

"It sure comes in handy," I said. "I use it for my leather work, too."

"Suppose you could show me how to make things out of leather?"

"I could," I said, surprised. "Anytime. Be glad to."

Do you know what, Grandma? Amos held out his hand and shook mine. Can you imagine that? Then, as Amos followed his father and Grandma Woodward to their car, he turned, smiled, and waved to me.

Pa and I headed back toward our house. "Say, George," Pa said, "how'd you get over here so fast? I thought you were going after the cows in the far pasture."

"I ran," I said.

"But I thought you couldn't run." Pa said. I answered that I had thought that, too, but I surprised myself. I hadn't realized how much better my leg has gotten. I felt better than I've felt in a long time.

I hope you can come to visit us yet this summer, Grandma. There are so many things I want to show you and a bunch of people I want you to meet. This farm is really a nice place.

Love,
George

Dear George,

Oh, my, what a lot of ups and downs you have had during the past few weeks. I'm glad you like the pencils and writing paper I sent. Your letters mean more than you will ever know.

And happy birthday, once again. Just think, you are thirteen years old, a young man. I wish I could have been with you on your fishing trip. It sounds like it was lots of fun, except for falling in the lake. I'm not sure I would have liked that. It sure was a big fish you caught, though.

I guess I predicted that Amos would find a way to pick a fight with you. I'm glad that neither of you got hurt badly. A black eye is no fun, but it could have been worse. There is just no sense in fighting. No sense at all. I'm sure you are well aware of that now.

As for the fire at Grandma Woodward's house, you, young man, are a hero. You can't know how proud I am of you. And I'll bet you a nickel that you have a new friend. His name is Amos Woodward.

I will see you in just a week. I've checked the train schedule and look forward to seeing all of you on August 27, at the depot in Link Lake. Be sure to bring Depot along with you. I'm looking forward to seeing him along with the rest of your family. It has been a long, lonely spring and summer here in Cleveland. I'm so looking forward to spending some time in the country.

Much love,
Grandma S.

Afterword

THE IMPORTANCE OF LETTER-WRITING

Although today many people use email, text messaging, and other electronic means of keeping in touch, letter-writing is an important form of communication. Writing a letter gives you time to develop an idea or thought or share a story of any length. Letters can be long or short, depending on what you want to say. Besides providing you a way to share your ideas with someone, a written letter becomes a historical record. A historian might someday read a letter you wrote "way back when" to learn about what life was like when you were growing up.

KINDS OF LETTERS

· In this book you've had a chance to read personal letters. George is writing to his grandmother, and she is writing back to him. They are informative, friendly, and valued by the person receiving them.

· Many people send letters on special occasions. Birthdays and other holidays are a fun reason to write a letter and send along a picture you have drawn or a project from school.

· A thank-you letter is a great way to tell someone thanks for a present or for doing something nice for you. Thank-you letters are often short, but they are very much appreciated by the recipient.

· In a request letter, the letter writer is asking for something. When you apply for a job, writing a letter is often a part of that process. Another kind of request letter might ask for a donation for a good cause.

LETTER-WRITING EXERCISES

· Just as George did in this book, write letters to your grandparents. Tell them what you've been doing in school and at home. They will love receiving your letters and will probably be excited to write back to you.

· Write a letter to a cousin who lives in another city. Tell your cousin what you are studying in school, what books you are reading, and what it is like living where you live.

· Do you have a friend who has moved away or changed schools? Having a pen pal is a fun way to keep in touch and learn about life in a different place. The letters will help you continue your friendship until you can see each other again.

· Write to the author of one of your favorite books. Tell the writer what you like about the book and what it means to you. You might even mention some of the things you didn't like about the book! Authors like to hear from their readers.

· Write to the president of the United States about an issue or problem in your school or community that you feel strongly about.

· Write a letter to your school principal or the mayor of your city. Describe a change or an improvement you think is needed and explain why.

· Write a letter to students who will be in your grade next year. Tell them about the classes they will have, the homework they should expect, and what you like about being in your grade (and what you don't like, as well).

If you are already writing letters, keep it up! Writing a letter is not only fun, it is an important skill to have.